THE GOOD GUY

Nicola Marsh

Kristen Lewis leads a glamorous life in Singapore as an executive producer of an exciting travel show. She's driven, focussed, and never gives in to impulse; like a one night stand with a sexy stranger.
After being head-hunted by an Australian TV studio, she's shocked to discover her new boss is the guy who rocked her world for that one memorable night.

Nathan Boyd is a billionaire entrepreneur. Focussing on work is the only way he knows how to cope with his grief. When he discovers Kris, the first woman to capture his attention in a long time, is now working alongside him, he's shocked.

When Kristen reveals her secret to Nathan, she becomes embroiled in a drama that belongs onscreen.
Will Nate be able to face his fear and take a chance on them?

Copyright © Nicola Marsh 2021
Published by Parlance Press 2022

All the characters, names, places and incidents in this book have no existence outside the imagination of the author and have no relation whatsoever to anyone bearing the same name or names and are used fictitiously. They're not distantly inspired by any individual known or unknown to the author and all the incidents in the book are pure invention. Any resemblance to actual events, locales, or persons, living or dead, is coincidental.

All rights reserved including the right of reproduction in any form. The text or any part of the publication may not be reproduced or transmitted in any form without the written permission of the publisher.

The author acknowledges the copyrighted or trademarked status and trademark owners of the word marks mentioned in this work of fiction.

First Published by Harlequin Enterprises in 2008 as EXECUTIVE MOTHER-TO-BE
World English Rights Copyright © 2021 Nicola Marsh

One

Kristen Lewis had a thing for hotels.

She loved the luxury, the hustle and bustle, even those tiny toiletries designed to slather and splurge and make a weary soul feel like a million dollars for that split second in time.

But most of all she loved the anonymity, where people from all walks of life passed each other without knowing or caring why a successful, thirty-five year old woman at the top of her game would be sitting alone at a bar sipping a spritzer.

"Men," she muttered, stabbing at the lemon wedge in her glass with a swizzle stick, wondering if the ability to blow off other people was a genetic thing. Even as friends they couldn't be trusted.

She took another stab at the piece of lemon, which was starting to resemble Swiss cheese with the number of jabs she'd taken at it in the last five minutes, as she glanced around the bar of the Jazz Hotel in Singapore.

She loved this place, with its sleek chrome lines, trendy black furniture and the occasional splash of red, and had spent many hours here with clients and work colleagues during her four year stint working at a Singaporean TV station. The hotel's grandeur screamed 'special occasion', the reason why she'd chosen to meet Nigel here tonight, envisioning a fun evening with her best work buddy when she'd share her amazing news. Unfortunately, Nigel had a better offer from a twenty-two year old temp and had given her the brush off in the foyer without even hearing her news.

"Buddy my butt," she muttered, taking a sip of her favourite white wine and soda combo as her gaze locked with a guy sitting at the other end of the bar.

Not bad. Dark eyes, dark hair, slight bump in the nose adding character to his handsome face, and sardonic expression highlighted by a slight quirk of his lips at the corners. Almost in a silent challenge, one she had no intention of accepting.

She lowered her gaze quickly and returned to studying coasters while mentally listing Nigel's faults, the main one being he'd ditched her for a temp rather than celebrating the news she'd be returning to Australia shortly. Not that she should be surprised. If Nigel had a choice between wining and dining his latest prospective conquest or sharing a drink with a friend, she lost every time.

Her gaze swept the bar again in and unerringly zeroed in on the good-looking guy. From past experience guys who looked like that sitting alone at a bar made eye contact before moving in for the kill and that's the last thing she needed in her current mood.

Instead, Mr. Handsome stared morosely into his drink, a sombre expression on his striking face and crazily, she sighed in disappointment. She'd never believed in fate or karma or any of that airy-fairy rubbish, yet when she'd locked gazes with the guy a few moments ago something intangible had zinged between them.

Now he wore the same brooding, gloomy expression that

matched her mood perfectly and for an irrational second she wondered if she should go over there and share sob stories with him.

With a shake of her head, she finished her spritzer—had to be more wine than soda in it for her to be contemplating such an uncharacteristic action—and scrummaged in her handbag for money.

"Is this yours?"

Looking up from the giant cavernous hole that sucked up purses, tissues, pens, makeup and everything else she needed on a daily basis, making them vanish with a flick of its clasp, she stared into the darkest eyes she'd ever seen, a dark chocolate bordering on black. The stranger she'd made eye contact with earlier now stared at her with polite interest.

"Is this your coat?" His voice, as deep and mysterious as his eyes, washed over her and she blinked, realising he waited for an answer.

"Yes, thanks." She stood, unable to look away, lost in his hypnotic stare.

He had to be pulling some slick, practised move on her and she didn't tolerate guys like that. So why was she standing like a mannequin, stiff and wide-eyed, unable to shake the feeling this guy was on her wavelength.

Smiling, he pointed to the floor. "You knocked it off the back of your stool while searching in that suitcase of yours."

"Suitcase?"

If his eyes mesmerised, they had nothing on his smile, which had her surreptitiously leaning against the bar for support. He pointed to her handbag. "Looks big enough to store the odd suit and a pair of shoes or two."

She laughed and snapped the 'suitcase' shut. "I'm on the go a lot so like to have everything at my fingertips. Important stuff like pens and notebooks and all the other paraphernalia I couldn't possibly find anywhere if I left all this at home."

His smile widened at her sarcasm but somehow it didn't reach his eyes, a flicker of sadness darkening their depths to almost black and she felt another twinge, an uncharacteristic urge to reach out and comfort him. "Speaking of being on the go, I should catch some sleep. I've got an early plane to catch tomorrow."

"Are you here on business?"

"Yes."

"I live here," she blurted, filled with a desperate urge to keep him talking, to find out more about the mysterious guy who saved her coat from death-by-trampling yet wore an invisible cloak of sadness around his broad shoulders.

"Really? By your Aussie accent I assumed you're here on business too?"

"I could be on holiday," she said, hating the stilted stand up conversation they were having, exactly why she didn't hang out at places like this.

"You're not on holiday."

She raised an eyebrow, surprised by his matter of fact tone. "How do you know that?"

"Because holiday makers have a relaxed look about them, an excited glow, and you don't have it."

"Gee, thanks. So I've lost my glow too," she muttered, wondering what she was doing making small talk with a guy she didn't know and who'd only stopped because she was a klutz.

"You've got a glow," he said, in a tight, strangled tone that made her look up and register the fleeting interest in his eyes. "Just not a holiday one."

Kristen didn't know if it was her bruised ego courtesy of being stood up by Nigel, the spritzer she'd had on an empty stomach, or the nebulous connection she felt for this sad stranger, but she found herself doing something completely out of character.

"If you're not too tired and can hold off on sleep a while longer, maybe you'd like to hear about my non-holiday glow?"

He didn't move, surprise mingling with something else—regret, hope, desire?—in his eyes and she wished the ground would open up as heat surged into her cheeks.

"Forget it. I'm sure you have more important things—"

"I'd like that," he said, hanging her coat over the back of the stool before sliding it out for her.

"Great." She sat, baffled by the simple pleasure derived from his acceptance.

"Would you like a drink?"

"A lemon, lime and bitters, please."

If the splash of wine in the spritzer was responsible for her erratic behaviour, she'd better stick to the soda, otherwise no telling what she might do.

After placing their order with the waiter—who had a knowing smile like he'd seen this scenario a thousand times before—the guy turned to her.

"I'm Nate."

She held out her hand. "Kris. Non-holiday maker. Living in Singapore and loving it."

Warmth enveloped her hand as he shook it with a solid grip. She liked that, hating when guys gave her a limp handshake because of her sex, though she usually showed them, turning their condescension into awe when she wowed them in the business arena.

"Are you living here with family?"

She shook her head, wondering if he was fishing for info about a significant other before ditching the idea. Nate seemed too up-front to play those sorts of games. If he were interested in her romantically he would've asked and sadly, she had a feeling he was sitting here chatting to her out of pity rather than desire for her as a woman. Something in the way he looked at her when she'd invited him to share a drink had clued her in, as if he'd like to refuse but didn't want to hurt her feelings.

She didn't care. Right now, it felt good to talk to someone—she'd been bursting with her news earlier—especially with a guy who looked like Nate, regardless of his motivations for hanging out with a sad case like her.

"No, I don't have much family. Two sisters back in Sydney, that's it. I've been here working, producing one of Singapore's travel shows."

"Sounds interesting."

He thanked the waiter as their drinks were placed in front of them and signed the bill slip, giving her ample opportunity to study him.

White business shirt unbuttoned at the collar and rolled up at the sleeves revealing strong forearms, shirt tucked into the waistband of black trousers encasing long legs ending in a pair of designer shoes. However, the clothes weren't the interesting part, it was the body beneath: lean, streamlined, hinting at subtle strength.

Usually, she wouldn't have given this stranger the time of day let alone invited him to share a drink, yet there was something haunting about Nate, an underlying vulnerability that had her wanting to cuddle him close and pat him comfortingly on the back.

"Can I ask you something?"

Her gaze snapped up from somewhere in the vicinity of his collar, where it parted to reveal a tantalising V of tanned skin, an expanse of skin she found infinitely fascinating for no other reason than what it hinted at.

"Sure."

"You were muttering into your drink earlier. Is everything okay?"

Once again, heat seeped into her cheeks. Could this get

any more embarrassing, the gallant guy having a pity drink with the desperate ditched?

"You know what they say about talking to yourself being the first sign of madness? Well, I'm mad all right. Mad enough to want to throttle my buddy Nigel for bailing on me."

"Ouch." Nate winced and she squared her shoulders, ready to rebuff his pity. Instead, she saw a glimmer of amusement lighting his eyes. "Did he stand you up?"

"Sure did, the jerk. Said he had a better offer from this girl he's been chasing for a while, so he ditches a friend. Nice."

"Very poor form," Nate said, his eyes twinkling beneath a mock frown. "Friends should always come first."

He was making light of her situation and rather than being insulted, laughter bubbled within her at the big deal she'd made out of something pretty insignificant. "Why did you think he stood me up?"

Nate's amusement spread to his mouth as it tilted up at the corners. "Well, if I'd taken one look at that giant bag and the maniacal gleam in your eyes, I would've made a run for it too."

She laughed, surprised the annoyance of being stood up by Nigel had receded, only to be replaced by a surprising need to swap banter with this guy.

"But you didn't make a run for it. You're sitting here."

"Good point." He tipped his glass in her direction before taking a long sip of beer, his gaze never leaving hers.

She couldn't figure him out. He wasn't flirting, making suggestive comments, or hinting at anything untoward, but when he stared at her like that—steady, unwavering, loaded— the air between them sizzled with an invisible current and had her reaching for her drink which she gulped in record time.

"You know it's his loss, right?"

Breaking the hypnotic eye contact, she said, "Yeah, I know. The guy's got his priorities all wrong."

"So he wasn't the love of your life?"

Kristen snorted, unable to picture scruffy, laid-back Nigel as anything other than a colleague she could offload to at the end of a rough day.

"No way. Nigel and I are purely platonic."

"Then he's definitely not worth worrying about now. You can give your friend an earful when you next see him."

"Too right." Considering how trivial her complaint against Nigel was, she wanted to know more about the sadness she'd glimpsed in Nate when she first saw him. "What about you? Any life stories to tell?"

If she'd doused him in her icy drink she would've got the same response: shock combined with pain, sorrow quickly masked by an enforced blank mask.

"Not really. I'm married to my job; don't have time for anything else."

"I know the feeling," she said, trying to cover her monstrous gaff in prying. "So what do you do?"

He hadn't lost his shuttered expression and he waited before speaking as if weighing every word. "I'm involved in the entertainment area too, though on the company side of things."

"So you're one of the corporate bigwigs who control the purse strings, right?"

At last, a glimmer of a smile. "You could say that. I'm the CEO of my own company and apart from handling sporting rights, we branch into other areas too."

"Well, if I ever need a job I'll know who to approach," she said, hating how her mind immediately latched onto his 'handling other areas' and conjuring up startling images of him doing exactly that...with her.

"You do that." He drained his beer and she braced for the inevitable parting, totally confused by her reticence to let him go.

She didn't know this guy.

She didn't want this to end.

She didn't have the foggiest idea what to do.

"I'm hungry after that beer. Do you want to join me for dinner?"

Trying to hide her relief—and elation—she said, "That would be great. The buffet here is the best in Singapore."

"So I've heard. Come on, let's try it."

Sliding off her stool, Kristen ignored her voice of reason yelling 'what do you think you're doing, having dinner with a guy you barely know? Are you nuts?'

"I don't usually do this type of thing," he said, handing her the infamous coat. "Having dinner with women I just met."

"That makes two of us."

Happily ignoring her voice of reason, she sent him a shy smile and fell into step beside him as they headed for the restaurant.

Two

Nate forked a delicious combination of spicy black pepper crab and fried rice into his mouth, trying to concentrate on the amazing food on his plate rather than the intriguing woman sitting across the table from him.

What am I doing here?

He'd asked himself the same question repeatedly over the last half hour and still hadn't come up with an answer. One that made sense, that is. He didn't chat up women, he didn't accept drink invitations, and he sure as hell didn't have dinner with them unless it involved business, yet here he was sharing the best meal he'd had in ages with a beautiful woman he'd known for less than an hour. And enjoying it.

"The food's good?"

He nodded, his gaze fixed on her mouth and the way her lips wrapped around a crab claw, his groin tightening with the sheer eroticism of the movement.

This couldn't be happening. He usually didn't have the time or the inclination. So what was he doing fantasising about this almost-stranger's lush mouth and what it would feel like on him?

"I'm a seafood addict," Kris said, dabbing at her glistening mouth with a serviette while he wrenched his mind out of the gutter. "This place is famous for it."

"Along with the roast duck, tandoori chicken, satays and the million other dishes on offer, you mean?"

She smiled, the power of that one simple action staggering in its ability to capture his interest and keep him riveted. "Wait until you try the desserts."

He didn't have a sweet tooth but at her suggestion he couldn't wait to try a chocolate mousse or lychee sorbet. He'd go along with anything this fascinating woman had to say at the moment, which showed exactly how jet-lagged he must be.

He needed to stop these two day jaunts to Asia if this was the result: a confused, half-drugged state that had him focussing on all the wrong cues, like the way her stunning blue eyes sparkled, how the highlights in her short, layered blonde hair shone, and the way her smile lit up the room.

As for her body—tall, lithe and graceful in the slim pinstripe skirt and pale blue shirt—he'd been struggling not to stare since he'd first seen her hunched over that gigantic bag of hers at the bar with her jacket in a crumple at her feet.

She'd appeared deliciously rumpled and flustered when he'd picked up her coat and nothing like the ice-cool blonde who'd locked gazes with him a minute before with her big sad eyes and grim expression.

He'd watched her for a while—toying with her drink, stabbing at the lemon wedge, her mouth muttering words he couldn't hear. He would've laughed if her expression hadn't been so fragile and though he had his own problems to deal with he'd been unable to walk past her without reaching out and giving her some indication she wasn't alone in the world, some indication he understood.

Boy, did he understand.

People said grief eased with time, that time healed all wounds.

People didn't know jack.

"Dessert is optional. You don't have to try if you'd rather not."

Hating that his mask had slipped for a moment and she must've glimpsed some of what he was feeling, he said, "Sorry, just thinking."

"About something not very pleasant by the looks of it?"

The question hung between them, softly probing but intrusive nonetheless.

"Guess being away from home has me in a mood."

"Being homesick is the pits," she said, placing her serviette on the table and sitting back. "I missed Sydney like crazy when I first came here but you want to know the secret to getting past it?"

"Sure."

Leaning forward, she tapped the side of her nose as if about to depart a secret lost in time. "Orangutans."

Maybe the jet lag was worse than he thought? He could've sworn she said something obtuse about monkeys.

She nodded, a smile playing about her mouth. "You heard me. Orangutans. The biggest, goofiest guys on the planet. You can't help but love them. I was feeling pretty lousy my first week here so I took a trip to the Singapore Zoo and spent an hour with the hairy goofballs, having breakfast with them, laughing at their antics. Suddenly, no more homesickness. Instant cure just like that."

She snapped her fingers and he blinked, wondering what it was about this cool yet kooky woman that had him so captivated.

"I'll keep that in mind," he said, shaking his head in disbelief, torn between wanting to bolt from the table before she enthralled him any further and hauling her into his arms to see if she was real.

She flittered between serious and funny, sad and happy, changing emotions like the frenetic activity of the stock market on opening. He hardly knew a thing about her yet he wanted to know more. He didn't know her surname yet he knew she loved seafood, had a brain behind her beauty, and had a thing for big monkeys.

They had little in common yet he knew he didn't want this evening to end.

He wanted to know more. If he were completely honest with himself, he wanted her with a staggering fierceness that clawed at him, begging to be released and soothed by her touch, in her arms, all night.

"Uh-oh, you're having more of those unpleasant thoughts." She picked up the wine bottle and topped up his glass, as if a fine Shiraz would fix what ailed him.

If it were that easy he would've bought out every vineyard in Australia by now.

Direct to the point of bluntness in business, he took a deep breath, opting for the same approach now and hoping it wouldn't earn him a slap.

"Actually, my thoughts aren't so unpleasant."

"Oh?" Her eyebrow kicked up, highlighting the curious glint in her blue eyes.

"I know this is going to sound crazy and you have every right to walk away from this table, but I was thinking we have a connection and I don't want this evening to end."

Surprise flashed across her face, closely followed by indignation? Fear? Hope? He had no idea. It had been a long time since he'd spent this much time with a woman let alone tried to fathom her emotions.

"Are you asking me to spend the night with you?"

He tried not to cringe at her bluntness Looked like he wasn't the only one who favoured the direct approach.

"I don't know what I'm asking," he muttered, eyeing the door and wondering if it was too late to make a run for it. "I don't do this very often. Hell, I haven't been out with a woman for years. But I know one thing. I'm attracted to you. You make me feel good. And I don't want to lose this feeling no matter how temporary."

It was as simple as that. No more, no less. This stunning woman with her expressive eyes and lush mouth had him feeling good for the first time in a long time and he wanted more.

"I think you do know what you're asking," she said, her gaze locked on his, her smile uncertain as she toyed with the ends of the tablecloth, twisting the damask over and over. "I think we both do and my answer is yes."

"Yes?" He exhaled, unaware he'd been holding his breath, filled with elation and anticipation and countless emotions he couldn't describe as she stared at him with excitement glittering in her expressive eyes.

"Yes."

From that moment everything faded into oblivion as he stood, held out his hand and felt an electrifying jolt as she placed hers in it, and led her from the restaurant to the lifts leading up to his room.

They didn't speak.

They didn't need to.

Words seemed superfluous as they entered his room, closed the door and fell into each others arms like two drowning people hanging on to the last life buoy: desperate, frantic, caught up in a storm bigger than the both of them.

As her lips clung to his and he deepened the kiss, his arms sliding around her waist to press her closer, a thrill shot through him.

He'd never done anything so rash, so reckless, so damn impulsive, and it felt good.

It felt great.

Thanks to the beautiful woman in his arms, he realised it was time to start living again.

Three

Kristen never did anything on impulse.

She never understood the rash decisions people made on the spur of the moment and then lamented later. She was a thinker who weighed options carefully, for everything from buying a pair of killer black stilettos to hiring the best grip boy.

Yet here she was lying next to the sexiest guy she'd ever met after having amazing sex. Twice.

Logical? No.

Well thought out? Uh-uh.

Satisfying, cataclysmic and exciting? Hell yeah.

Wriggling under the cotton sheet covering them, she stretched, tensing every muscle from her toes to her fingers before relaxing, savouring the warm, sated sensation creeping through her tired body.

To say she'd never felt like this before would be the understatement of the year.

Risking a quick glance at him, she smiled, lost in delicious memories of how he'd kissed her, held her, and made love to her with every inch of his body, and corny as it may sound she knew it had been more than a physical connection.

Inexplicably, they'd clicked. For whatever reason, whether it be his underlying vulnerability, his innate sadness, or the fact he was a refined, well-mannered, genuinely nice guy, she'd thrown caution to the wind and had sex with a virtual stranger.

She should be mortified or cringing with embarrassment. Instead, she rolled onto her side and watched him sleep, calm filling her with warmth. With his lips relaxed in a half smile and his long dark eyelashes fanning his cheeks, he looked a lot younger than when he was awake and carrying around the inherent sadness like a back-pack weighing him down.

What would make a successful guy who looked like he could model underwear on billboards around the world so sad? Guys his age with money to burn were usually chasing women, striving for the next big thing and whooping it up in general, not necessarily in that order. She should know, she mixed in those circles and held those players at arms length constantly.

Yet here was a guy who probably moved in that social sphere wearing his sadness like a badge of honour. He seemed lonely, not that she knew anything beyond the basics about him. Heck, she didn't even know his surname. However, there was something about him...she hadn't conjured up their connection out of thin air. It was there, it was real, and for the last few hours everything had faded into the background while she hooked up with a kindred spirit.

"You're awake."

She blinked and focused on Nate, smiling at his heavy-lidded, sleepiness. "Can't sleep. Guess I'm not used to sharing my bed."

Not that it bothered her. She valued her independence

and hated having to fight over the duvet with a guy hogging half the bed.

"Whose bed?" He smiled, his tone soft and husky, washing over her like a warm spring shower and making her want to throw her arms wide and dance in the sheer beauty of it.

"Good point. Make that *your* bed," she said, wondering how this could feel so right.

She'd expected a tense, awkward conversation on waking, perhaps the odd excuse or two. Instead, they lay there, grinning at each other like a couple of goofy teenagers, barely inches apart, naked.

"You're okay with all this, right?" His smile waned as the light in his eyes faded and she braced for the 'this was a mistake, see you round' chat.

She nodded, making sure her smile didn't slip. "Of course. I wouldn't be here if I didn't want to be. We're two consenting adults who made a decision to spend the night together. No big deal."

Then why the emptiness behind her words? Or the hollowness in her heart when she had no right to feel anything other than physical attraction for this guy?

"You're right," he said, dropping his gaze to her hand bunching the sheet and she relaxed with effort.

He may agree with her mature, rational assessment of a potentially awkward situation but his guilty expression said otherwise. Which made her wonder...why did he feel guilty? He was single—she'd made sure of it before she entered his hotel room. Then again, it wouldn't be the first time a guy lied to get a woman into bed. But she prided herself on being a good judge of character and Nate didn't seem the sleazy type.

When he frowned, she could've reached out to him and prompted him to tell her what was wrong but she didn't have the right. Apart from sharing one fabulous night of scintillating sex and an unexpected connection, she didn't know him, not enough for him to confide in her.

Wanting to ease the sadness now mingling with the guilt on his expressive face, she said, "Look, I don't usually do this sort of thing and by your reaction I'm guessing it's the same for you?"

He raised his gaze slowly upwards, remorse darkening his eyes to almost black. "I never do this. Does it show?"

Great, now he thought she'd insulted his prowess. She reached out and covered his hand with hers, hoping the simple physical contact would convey half of what she was feeling.

"Last night was fabulous. I just meant dealing with all this aftermath stuff is kind of icky."

"Icky, huh?" His lips twitched and she silently congratulated herself for bringing the semblance of a smile to his face.

Returning his smile, she said, "I guess what I'm trying to say is you've got nothing to feel bad about. We both wanted to be with each other last night, let's leave it at that."

His smile flickered as something akin to shame flashed in his eyes and she knew she'd somehow said the wrong thing again.

"You're an incredible woman, Kris. Thank you for last night."

He cupped her cheek, his thumb brushing her bottom lip in the slowest, tender, barely there movement before letting go, leaving her wanting more, craving his touch when she hardly knew it.

This wasn't good. She was neither drunk nor stupid so lying here lost in useless wishes of 'what may be' was pointless.

Nate had a plane to catch and a life to get back to, she had a new job in Australia to look forward to. Time to start looking to the future and chalk up this incredible encounter to a fate she didn't believe in.

"Thank you," she said, brushing a hasty kiss across his lips before slipping out of bed, clutching the sheet around her. "You have a plane to catch in a few hours so I'll leave you to it."

"Kris?"

She paused, wishing she could skip the farewell and fast-forward to a month from now when she'd be back on solid ground, away from the seductive powers of a virtual stranger in an exotic place, caught up in the type of magical romance she knew didn't exist in the real world.

"Yes?"

Nate stared at her, his dark, intense gaze trying to send her a message she couldn't fathom. His sad mask had slipped back into place and for a split second she wondered if their impending goodbye had anything to do with it.

Yeah, like he'd be heartbroken over a woman he barely knew.

"I wish things were different."

For one, heart-stopping moment she felt the same zing, the same spark she had back in the bar when they'd first met, the same tenuous connection implying this was meant to be, and she almost ran back to the bed and flung herself into his arms.

But that wasn't the sensible thing to do and right now logic was about all she had left.

"I do too," she finally said, opting for honesty yet knowing it wouldn't make a difference as she slipped into the bathroom to get dressed and head back to her well-organised life and out of his.

Four

Kris strode to the shiny chrome desk of Channel RX feeling like the new kid on the block and hating it. No matter how confident she was or how carefully she power-dressed, the same terrifying insecurity that had swamped her every time she'd started a new school or been introduced to a new foster family would return. She loathed it.

Determinedly quelling her nerves, she flashed a brash smile, leaned on the desk and fixed the young receptionist with a confident stare. "Hi, I'm Kristen Lewis, the new executive producer."

The receptionist, a bright-eyed twenty-something, held up her hand as she fielded what looked like five calls at once and Kristen relaxed, feeling at home straight away. At least this wasn't any different. She could walk into any television studio around the world and find the same version of a harried receptionist, the flood of incoming calls from irate or scandalised viewers, and an addictive buzz on the studio floor.

She loved working in television: the drama, the rush, the constant push to be better and strive higher than the competition. She was good at what she did, which is why she'd been lucky enough to land this plum job at Melbourne's premier station. She couldn't wait to take up the challenge, something new to take her mind off Singapore and that fateful night she couldn't forget no matter how hard she tried.

"Right, sorry about that," the receptionist said. "I'm Hallie, general dogsbody around this place. Would you like to head on through or shall I call the boss and let him know you're here?"

"I'll find my own way, thanks. Give me a chance to look around."

Hallie flashed a relieved smile as she cast a frantic look at the phone ringing again. "No worries. If you need anything, holler."

Kristen waved and headed for the imposing black swing doors. This was it. The start of a new job, life in a new city, without memories of a guy with unforgettable dark chocolate eyes.

"Kristen?"

She stopped and swivelled to face Hallie. "Yes?"

"The boss man just buzzed through to ask if you'd arrived. He wants to see you in his office ASAP. Through the doors, down the corridor on your left, last office on the right."

"Thanks."

Kristen pushed through the doors and into the swankiest studio she'd ever seen. Faux polished floorboards lined the endless corridors stretching left and right with countless doors off each one, while a huge auditorium-like space enclosed in glass—with a small army of crew and extras swarming around a mock kitchen set—lay straight ahead.

No one stopped to stare at the newbie, not even the odd curious glance. She knew what it was like. Once the cameras rolled everyone performed their roles to perfection. The cameras didn't lie and the slightest mistake could cost a whole take or worse, be aired live to an unforgiving audience.

A tingle raised the hackles on her skin and she shivered. Damn, it was good to be back.

Feeling more confident with every passing second, she strode down the left corridor as instructed, resisting the urge to peek into every office. Many doors were open, the hum of voices and the smell of brewed coffee heavy in the air, and she hoped her new boss would offer her a cup. She'd kill for a caffeine hit right now, what with the move to Melbourne combining with her sleepless nights—courtesy of Mr. Handsome who she really hoped would turn into Mr. Forgettable any time now.

She knew nothing about her new boss. After being headhunted by a Channel RX producer while in Singapore, she'd barely had time to study the channel online let alone learn who the head honcho was, some new appointment that seemed to be the industry's best kept secret.

Thankfully, she rarely dealt with the CEO's of outfits like this: slick, go get 'em types who were focussed on the bottom dollar and little else. She'd much rather concentrate on the enjoyable task of creating great TV than counting cents to make it happen.

Reaching the final door on the right, she pulled up short.

NATHAN BOYD, CEO.

She blinked, hating the irrational surge of heat the name Nathan sent through her.

Damn it, she should be over this; over him. It had been one night months ago. One incredible, amazing night when she'd connected with a guy whose surname she didn't even know. Yeah, really connected.

Shaking her head, she wiped her damp palms against her skirt, tugged at her jacket hem and knocked on the door.

However, as the door opened and she willed her legs to

stay upright, Kristen knew forgetting Nate and that one eventful night would be impossible.

Considering Nathan Boyd, CEO, and her new boss, was her Nate.

The guy who had rocked her world.

Five

Nate's smile faded as Kristen tried her best not to reel back in shock. "Kris?"

Not the smoothest of opening lines from Nate but considering she couldn't think let alone form words at that moment he was faring a damn sight better than her.

Looking way too calm, he stepped aside and gestured her in. "Please come in."

She ignored his invitation, her legs rooted to the spot. Wasn't he the least bit rattled to find her in his office? How could he look so cool, so unflappable?

In that moment as she studied his composed face, she knew exactly why she'd been head-hunted for this job and by whom.

"I don't believe this," she said, years of professionalism deserting her as she stared at him in growing horror, heat surging to her cheeks.

"Come inside and we'll discuss it," he said, his voice as deep and steady as she remembered as he opened the door wider and waited for her to step inside.

She marched through the door like a woman sentenced to the gallows and collapsed into the nearest chair on the visitor's side of his desk, and took several calming breaths. "Did you know about this?"

He sat behind his desk, shoulders relaxed and arms resting comfortably on his fancy leather director's chair while she could barely keep a lid on her growing temper.

"About you working here? No."

"Really? I'm guessing there aren't a lot of executive producers named Kristen. Were you behind me being headhunted?"

"Why would you think that?"

Rolling her eyes, she said, "Come on, you're a smart man. Do I need to spell it out? Singapore? The night we were together?"

His lips thinned as he ran a hand through his hair, the first sign he was anything other than on top of the situation.

"I had no idea who the new exec producer was until I opened that door and saw you standing there. I've been in charge of this operation for less than twenty-four hours and have spent most of that time out on the studio floor. I haven't studied employee lists, haven't had the time." He glanced at his watch as if to emphasise it. "I asked Hallie to send along everyone from the top down at half hourly intervals so I can get acquainted face to face rather than studying boring CVs."

Her anger deflated with the sincerity in his voice as the reality of the situation hit her. She'd barged into her new boss's office with the finesse of a wounded rhino, flinging wild accusations and acting like the injured party when this was her dream job and she'd made a lousy first impression.

"I'm surprised *you* didn't do your homework. Study up on who you'd be working for." Nate fixed her with a stare she found disconcertingly familiar, a gleam of challenge in the dark depths of his eyes, and she bristled, hating his inference she wasn't professional.

"I did. Though I guess the contract I signed and the studio's website doesn't mention your name." She snapped her fingers, not willing to give an inch, her latent anger taking little to reignite. "Then again, I wouldn't have made the connection, not knowing your surname."

He stiffened, the faintest red staining his tanned cheeks. "You're over-reacting. You don't see me throwing around allegations like maybe you knew I was CEO here and wanted to disarm me by walking in here today as my newest employee?"

"Over-reacting?" She leaped from her chair before she could think twice, planting her hands on his desk and leaning forward. "Aren't you the least bit thrown by this bizarre situation? Don't you feel awkward? And do you honestly think I'd go to the trouble of faking a shocked reaction to get a rise out of you?"

Shaking her head, she plopped back down in her chair, embarrassed by her outburst. "I'm sorry if I over-reacted but honestly? Finding you're my boss has thrown me."

Not half as thrown at how attracted to him she was even in a crazy situation like this. While she wanted to rant and rave at the injustice of having to work with a guy she'd rather forget, she couldn't help but admire his charcoal grey designer suit and the way it fit the great body she'd already had the pleasure of exploring in intimate detail.

As for his eyes, they were mesmerising, their darkness a fathomless pool of mystery begging to be explored and her pulse raced at the memories of how far she'd taken that exploration…

Sitting back, he clasped his hands behind his head, every bit the consummate professional, while she struggled to refocus her wandering attention and come to terms with her new employer.

"A coincidence over which I had no control. Now, what do you want to do?"

She wanted to walk out of his office and never look back. She wanted to stop noticing the way his business shirt stretched across his chest as he leaned back, the same hard, muscular chest she'd had one-on-one contact with. But most of all, she wanted to forget how he'd made her feel for one incredible night.

Taking a steadying breath, she said, "I want to be the best damn executive producer RX has ever had. But this is still uncomfortable." She waved her hands between the two of them, wishing he wouldn't look at her like that, the intensity of his dark gaze resurrecting memories she'd rather forget, her mind still reeling from the fact they'd be working together.

"It doesn't have to be. We're professionals. I'm sure what's happened in the past doesn't have to affect our work."

"Professionals. Right." Her shoulders relaxed, knowing she'd faced a lot hairier situations and come out on top. Besides, how hard could working with Nate be? "You're right. We didn't mind the anonymity that night and it's in the past. Done. Forgotten. So, Nathan Boyd, what's your vision for Channel RX and how do you see me fitting into it?"

Straight to the point and no bull. She valued bluntness in her employees and hoped he did too, especially considering her emotional outburst after she set foot in this office.

Thankfully, he accepted her switch back to professional and gathering a stack of papers in front of him, he shuffled a stapled bundle into a glossy navy folder and handed it to her.

"My vision's in there, laid out in black and white. I want Channel RX to be the best in Melbourne, with the aim to be number one in Australia within a year. I want ratings in prime time slots to soar, I want innovation, I want a fresh slant on old faithfuls such as the news and current affairs. In a nutshell? I want it all."

"You're aiming high," she said, a tiny thrill of excitement shooting through her at the thought of working with a boss who had a clear vision. "I like that."

Nodding, he clasped his hands and leaned forward. "As I haven't had a chance to find out from other sources yet, tell me what you bring to RX."

"That's easy. I'm the best."

She shrugged, knowing now wasn't time for modesty. She needed to impress Nate, to wow him, to show him what they'd shared really was in the past and she could give one hundred percent to the job despite her earlier uncharacteristic tantrum.

His lips twitched, resurrecting instant memories of how skilled they were at kissing, and she quickly subdued that train of thought. "You're very confident."

"I have to be in this business," she said, fixing him with a direct stare designed to convince him of her sincerity. "I love my job. I'm prepared to put in the long hours, to do whatever it takes to make the shows I work on successful. I demand respect and I treat co-workers the same way I'd like to be treated. I won't settle for second best. I deserve more than that."

"I think you're a great asset to this station." His lips curved into a genuine smile as he stood and held out his hand. "We're going to make a good team."

"Thanks." She shook his hand quickly, dropping it before she had time to register the quick surge of heat from his palm to hers. "I'll go find my office and get acquainted with the rest of the gang."

"Great. I'll see you later."

She headed for the door, wondering if this surreal experience was a dream and she'd wake up as soon as she stepped into the corridor.

"Kris?"

"Yes?"

Her hand stilled on the doorknob as her heart thudded with how he said her name, and the memories of how many times he'd murmured it that night in Singapore.

"It's good seeing you again."

Managing a strangled smile, she bolted out the door.

Six

Kristen willed her legs to move at a sedate pace as she walked away from Nate's office, when she wanted to bolt down the long corridor and keep running until she reached the massive front doors and beyond.

Seeing the guy she'd spent sleepless nights trying to forget open that office door had been like a slap in the face, a swift, sharp wake up call she hadn't forgotten him at all. More precisely, hadn't forgotten how he made her feel: feminine, desired and special.

How could he elicit those feelings when she barely knew him? How could she face him on a daily basis knowing he had that sort of power over her?

Rounding a corner, she pulled up short as Hallie held up her hands to stop a collision. "Hey, you okay?"

"Sure."

By Hallie's raised eyebrow, she didn't believe her. "Didn't the meeting with the boss go well?"

"It was fine."

As fine as being placed in her first foster family and finding her hopes of being part of a happy family shot down by their callous indifference.

"You look like you could use a coffee. I'm heading to the cafeteria. Want to join me?"

Kristen would've preferred to find her office and bury herself in work while getting her emotions under control but the lure of caffeine proved too strong. She needed something to jolt her out of the trance-like shock at finding Nathan was her new boss.

"Love to," she said, falling into step with Hallie, who stood a foot shorter than her but moved with surprising speed on three inch stilettos.

"What did you think of the boss?"

Kristen chose her words carefully. "Nathan seems like a man with a vision. The channel should go far."

"Nathan, huh?"

Hallie sent her a wink and Kristen battled a rising blush and failed, speaking quickly to cover her gaff. "He's very informal for a CEO. Actually, I didn't expect to meet him on the first day. The CEOs of stations I've worked at before don't get too hands on."

"The boss only started yesterday and if you want my opinion, he can get hands on with me any time."

"That's not very professional," Kris blurted, wishing she'd bitten her tongue as Hallie stared at her in wide-eyed confusion.

Thankfully, a group of cameramen greeting Hallie like a long lost friend diffused the moment. Besides, Kristen wasn't jealous. She had to care to be jealous and she didn't; she couldn't.

"Okay, here we are," Hallie said, waving off the boys and holding open the cafeteria door for her. "The coffee isn't bad if you don't mind the odd dreg or two."

Smiling at the receptionist's sense of humour, Kristen

followed her into a cavernous room filled with stainless steel tables and chairs, hot food piled high behind glass lining one wall and a huge selection of crisps, chocolate bars and sodas nearby.

By what she'd seen so far, Channel RX did things on a grand scale and if the videos of their current shows she'd watched before accepting the job had been any indication she'd made a wise choice.

"What'll it be? They do a mean latte and seeing as it's your first day, my shout."

"Latte's fine. And thanks," Kristen said, feeling like a chick being pushed around by a mother hen.

"Let's sit over there and you can tell me the Kristen Lewis story," Hallie said. "Back in a sec."

True to her word, Hallie returned in record time and handed her a steaming latte. "Now, tell me your story."

"Not much to tell," Kristen said, unable to resist Hallie's open friendliness but wary all the same. "Besides, if I tell you all my deep, dark secrets on the first day, you'll think I'm a gossip."

Hallie rolled her eyes. "Let's get a few things straight. There aren't a lot of women who work here, if you don't count the starlets and the anchor women who don't usually have the time of day for me. You're the first woman who's walked through the front doors and actually been polite let alone made eye contact so I'm bestowing you the great honour of being my work buddy."

Kristen didn't know what to say and before she could come up with something, Hallie held up her hand. "Don't thank me. I know it's a highly coveted position to be on the good side of the receptionist and you're probably shell-shocked but trust me, I'm nice."

Staring into Hallie's guileless blue eyes, registering her wide, friendly smile, Kristen knew she had one ally at RX.

Taking a sip of her surprisingly good latte, she said, "Are you always this upfront?"

Hallie nodded, her auburn curls bouncing around her face. "Yep. Only way to be. I know you're an exec and will probably blow me off after this, but hey, no harm in trying, right?"

"Actually, I've always been a bit of a loner on the job. Too tied up in my work, I guess. But I appreciate the coffee. If you let me know any time you're having one and I'm free, I promise not to blow you off. Deal?"

"Deal." Hallie settled back into her chair as if snuggling into a comfy sofa when Kristen assumed the hard, cold, steel chairs were meant to discourage occupants from getting too cosy and encouraging them to get back to work pronto. "So, what's your background?"

"I've worked in Singapore the last four years, London before that, brief stint in LA and Sydney, where I have an apartment. Worked my way up to executive producer through those jobs, loved every minute of it."

"Wow, sounds glamorous." Hallie's eyes lit up and Kristen wondered when she'd last had that wide-eyed interest in anything. "But you've basically given me a run down of your CV. What about your personal life? Any goss there?"

Determinedly ignoring a fleeting image of a naked Nate flashing across her mind, Kristen forced a laugh and made a zipping motion over her lips. "Not a morsel of scandal, I'm afraid. I'm a confirmed workaholic. Single and loving it."

Hallie sent her a dubious look but continued her questioning regardless. "Why Melbourne? Why RX?"

"The station has a stellar reputation in the industry, I wanted to come back to Australia and the opportunity was presented itself so I took it. Now, if you could spare me a minute in this interrogation I'd like to have this latte before it goes cold?"

She'd meant it as a joke but it looked like her buddy skills were on a par with her maintaining-a-relationship skills as Hallie's face fell. Damn, this was why she didn't make friends easily. Being direct was the only way she knew and treading around bruised feelings was foreign to her. Guess she better learn fast if she didn't want to alienate the one person who'd been genuinely nice to her.

"Sorry, I didn't mean to sound so harsh. I'm a bit strung out with the move to Melbourne and starting the new job."

"No worries," Hallie said, her resident cheery smile back in place. "I have to get back to work anyway. I'll save the rest of the interrogation for later."

"Later?"

Kristen had envisaged a long day getting acquainted with the running sheets, her co-workers, and the station in general. She had no time for further coffee breaks, especially ones fraught with probing questions from a girl trying to be friendly.

Hallie snapped her fingers. "I forgot, you probably don't know about Manic Mondays."

"Actually, I think I do," Kristen said, knowing the frantic rush of a new working week all too well.

She usually grabbed a bite to eat at her desk for dinner, working all hours to get the week's scheduling on track. It had been the same at every station around the world and it was comforting to know things weren't so different here.

"Bet you don't." Hallie's sly grin piqued her curiosity and she grabbed her latte-to-go, falling into step beside the petite receptionist.

"Okay, enlighten me."

"Every Monday the gang stops work at eight and convenes at our local pub for a bit of team bonding and morale boosting. It's great."

Taking time out of her busy schedule to have a drink at a

bar with co-workers on a Monday night? As if. "I'm sure it is but I'll be tied up tonight."

And for every Monday night while she worked here. She didn't casually socialise well, preferring to maintain a distance from work colleagues. Sharing a coffee with Hallie was a first and if the girl knew she'd probably label her a freak. Not that Kristen cared. She'd been labelled a heck of a lot worse growing up and she'd survived.

"I'm betting you're not tied up tonight," Hallie smirked as she held open the door and Kristen walked through.

"Why's that?"

Hallie leaned forward as if about to impart a trade secret. "Because Manic Mondays are company policy. Everyone attends, from the janitors to the CEO. It really does keep everyone happy. The first drink is on the house and if people want to stay around they do, but most folks have a drink or a coffee, a quick chat, then head home. It isn't a super late night and TPTB find it works as well as a bonus scheme for morale."

"Right," Kristen said, feeling like she was in quicksand and floundering.

Since when did The Powers That Be sanction weekly social get-togethers for employees let alone make it mandatory?

She'd have a chat to the CEO about this. Just as soon as she plucked up the courage to face him without wanting to fall into his arms.

Seven

Nathan sipped his espresso, content to lean against the bar—a suitable distance away from the RX crowd—and watch. He could learn a lot about people by the way they interacted with others and seeing his employees mingle and chat spoke volumes.

Like Hallie, the young receptionist whose bubbly personality won over everyone within two feet. And Alan, his second in command, who alienated people with his pompous ramblings, yet nobody moved away for fear of offending a bigwig.

Then there was Kristen, a fish out of water if ever he saw one. The erect posture, the fixed smile, the glazed look in her striking blue eyes and the way she kept casting furtive glances at the door, screamed she didn't want to be here.

He'd picked her as a fellow loner in Singapore but he expected a confident career woman like her to be more outgoing, more extroverted, yet she looked like she'd rather have teeth pulled rather than stand around and mix with her new workmates.

He drained his coffee, set the mug on the bar and made his

way towards the door. He'd done his duty, putting in an appearance when all he wanted to do was head home and read the pile of reports tucked into his briefcase and the latest ratings compilation on his laptop.

However, getting to the door put him straight in the pathway of the one woman he'd rather avoid and had done a good job of doing so far.

"Kristen," he said, terse to the point of rudeness. Idiot.

"Nathan."

Her polite nods and flat tone grated on his nerves, especially when she'd previously called him Nate. In Singapore, he'd surprised himself by telling her his name was Nate when it had been an abbreviation reserved for Julia and close family only, yet once it had slipped out he hadn't minded. He'd liked how natural it sounded coming from her, lending familiarity to what should've been a once-in-a-lifetime chance encounter.

Instead, here they were again, trying their utmost to act like they hadn't spent an incredible evening indulging in a surprising, all-consuming passion.

"Heading home?"

A simple question. So why did the way she said it conjure up unwelcome images of them heading home together? "Loads of work to do," he said. "You know how it is."

"I sure do," she said, a spark of understanding in her blue eyes creating an instant bond between them. "I guess we're both finding our feet in a new job, huh?"

He nodded, torn between escaping while he still could and staying a while longer in the hope to get their relationship—their working relationship—back on an even keel. "It's tough at the start but I actually love walking into a new place and starting fresh. It's a challenge."

Kris smiled, the first time he'd seen a genuine expression of joy since their fraught meeting earlier that day. "And let me guess, like any boss, you thrive on a challenge."

"Nothing wrong with that."

He returned her smile and their gazes locked. He should've looked away first but he couldn't, riveted by the tiny cerulean flecks in her blue eyes, remembering how they'd glowed and sparked when she'd been warm and eager in his arms.

Thankfully, she finally broke the deadlock with a little laugh. "No, there's nothing wrong with enjoying a challenge. I'm all for it myself."

"A fierce businesswoman, huh?"

"That's me." She raised her glass in his direction. "Don't say I didn't warn you."

"I stand duly warned," he said, looking forward to seeing what this dynamic woman could bring to his life. To his *professional* life.

She sipped her drink, a teasing glint in her eyes as she lowered it. "Good. Because I intend to put in long hours, do the hard yards, whatever it takes to propel RX to the top, just as my pushy boss wants in his vision statement."

He chuckled. "So you read the documents already? I'm impressed."

"You should be."

Her smile faded and he wondered at the turnaround, wishing he could recapture the easy-going camaraderie of the last few minutes.

"It's great to have an employee with a vision too. But won't long hours interfere with your family?"

Being involved with anything other than business came at a cost and he should know. He was still paying a steep price.

If her smile had faded moments before, the shutters well and truly descended now as her expression blanked. "I can't remember if I told you in Singapore but I only have two sisters. Carissa lives in Stockton, north of Sydney, and Tahnee lives in Sydney. They're both overseas travelling with their families at the moment so don't worry, I won't have any distractions."

"Sorry for being nosy," he said, the coldness in her voice sending a chill through him. So much for camaraderie. "Just trying to foster good employee relations."

"Don't worry about it," she said, waving off his apology but her flat tone told him he'd botched whatever inroads he'd made in getting her to unwind.

"On that note, I'm definitely heading off." Before he put his foot in it again and this time set her off like the wild woman who'd stormed into his office this morning.

"Actually, I think I'll head out myself. If it's okay for the boss to escape early, it's good enough for me," she said, her fragile smile creating a pocket of warmth deep within and he fell into step beside her, heading for the door.

She waved to Hallie, who eyed them with open speculation, and he held the door open for her, savouring the light rose scent he remembered all too well. It had lingered on his sheets after she'd left his hotel room, imprinted on his brain like the memory of what they'd shared.

"Would you like me to walk you to your car? Inner city Melbourne can be a bit dodgy at night," he said, surprised by a strong surge of protectiveness.

He hadn't felt that way towards a woman since Julia, what seemed eons ago now.

"My car's right here so I'll be fine, but thanks."

"Right. I'll see you tomorrow."

She nodded and crossed the road, an elegant figure in a fitted hounds' tooth power suit, sheer black stockings and towering heels. Dressed for business, she looked incredible, but as hard as he tried he couldn't forget how much more incredible her body was beneath the clothes.

Blinking away that unforgettable image, he waited until

she got into her snazzy two door, started the engine and pulled away from the kerb, returning her brief wave as she drove by.

He watched her tail-lights glow red in the distance, like two glittering eyes pinning him with an accusatory stare, a reminder that while he may be trying to establish a working relationship with Kris, he couldn't forget that one night of passion they'd shared.

Eight

"Kris, can you come in here please?"

Throwing down her pen on the stack of scripts in front of her, Kristen glared at the intercom phone on her desk, hating the thing more than her phone, considering both had become an instant connection to Nate and his demands.

She poked her tongue out at the machine before she hit the answer button.

"Be right there," she said, pushing away from her desk and grabbing her writing pad and the latest updates on new shows, knowing that no matter how prepared she was her new boss would find something to trump her with.

Heading down the long corridor to his office, she acknowledged at several co-workers, amazed she'd only been here four days when it felt like a lifetime. Familiarity bred that feeling. It also bred contempt, which she was fast heading towards if Nate didn't lighten up.

She knocked on his door and when he yelled, "Come in," she forced a smile and strode into his office.

"You wanted to see me, boss?"

His head snapped up like she'd called him something far worse—not entirely out the question considering how grumpy he'd been the last few days—and he frowned.

"Take a seat. I need to discuss something with you."

"No problems." She sat opposite him, stacking her pile of scripts on her lap and doing her best to appear perky and upbeat, hoping it would reinforce how grouchy he was.

Sitting back in his chair, he crossed his arms, and she struggled not to notice the way his biceps bulged beneath his pale blue business shirt. In a way, having him act like a pain in the ass was better than having him joking around with her like on Monday night when it had felt way too comfortable standing in a crowded bar with the man she couldn't forget no matter how hard she tried.

"I want to run an idea past you."

"Shoot," she said, clicking her pen and automatically sliding her writing pad to the top of the pile on her lap. She always brainstormed on paper and had been teased by younger colleagues who worked exclusively on electronic devices.

"You remember we discussed a new travel show on Tuesday?"

"Uh-huh."

How could she forget? They'd been holed up in his office brainstorming ideas for new shows and she'd been determined to impress on her second day on the job, well aware of her expertise in the travel show area. However, what she hadn't been prepared for was the host of memories continually scattering across her mind at the most inopportune time: talk of travel with him resurrected Singapore moments, Jazz Hotel moments, long, hot, exquisite moments with Nate...

"I've given it a lot of thought and I want us to run with it. See what you can come up with and we'll meet to discuss it on Monday."

"Fine," she said, unable to keep a huge self-satisfied smile off her face, only to find him glaring at her like she'd thrown a glass of cold water over him. "What time?"

He reached for his phone, checked the calendar, and frowned. "The earliest I can do is four-thirty. I'm in Brisbane until then."

"Sounds good," she said, making a show of checking her calendar but knowing she'd shift any meeting to demonstrate to her uptight boss what she could do. "Anything else?"

She was laying it on a little thick with her sweeter-than-honey smile and saccharine voice but the more intimidating he got the more she wanted to push him. She enjoyed a challenge and she had warned him.

He stared at her, his dark eyes revealing nothing, but she could've sworn she saw the corners of his mouth twitch. But that meant he wanted to laugh and there was no way her serious boss would actually crack a smile during work hours.

Shaking his head, he said, "No, that's it. See you Monday."

"Have a good trip."

Striding to the door, she put an extra swivel into her hips, grateful she'd worn her tightest black skirt today. If Nate wanted to treat his new exec producer with cold indifference, she'd give him a bit of a shake-up and show him that he hadn't always been impervious towards her. Unprofessional, maybe, but she hated the frigid working relationship they'd slipped into. She may prefer to keep her colleagues at a distance but Nate was taking the cool approach to extremes.

Swivelling at the door, she caught him staring at her butt a split second before his gaze snapped up to meet hers and his residual frown slipped into place.

"Was there something else?"

Fighting a triumphant grin that she'd finally got some kind of reaction out of him, she said, "Never mind. We'll discuss it further on Monday," a promise she had no intention of keeping.

They needed to stay work-focussed, but for that brief second when she'd seen him staring at her butt and the flash of remembrance in his eyes, she'd remembered how amazing it felt when Nate let down his guard and lost control.

NINE

"This is it?" Nate's eyebrows rose as he flicked through the documentation Kristen had prepared, his expression carefully schooled into a blank mask that gave nothing away.

"That's what I've come up with so far. I wanted to outline the gist of the show, run through a few preliminaries with you before getting too involved. What with budgets being the be all and end all, I'd like to see what you think before taking it further."

He nodded and rubbed his chin absentmindedly, flicking the last page and finally glancing at her. "It looks good. I particularly like the reality show slant you've put on it. It's something new and innovative, exactly the direction I want RX to be heading. Great job, Kris."

She smiled, instantly forgetting how less than five minutes earlier she'd wanted to pick up the fancy letter opener on his desk and stab him with it considering he'd been an hour and a half late, had waltzed in here with his usual sore head, and proceeded to read her proposal in silence without giving a clue to what he thought.

"I'm pretty excited about it, as you can probably tell," she said, pointing at the giant stack of paper she'd prepared to wow him with.

Tapping his pen on the stack, he said, "I'm amazed you did all this since Thursday."

"Once I got going I couldn't stop."

Wasn't that the truth, considering she'd spent her entire weekend preparing this presentation rather than enjoying the Melbourne sunshine.

"When you said long hours you meant it."

He made it sound like a fault and she bristled.

"I'm a professional. I thought you'd gathered that by now."

A spark of awareness flared in his eyes as he registered her dig.

"Your work speaks for itself," he said, staring at her for longer than was comfortable before slamming the stack of paper in front of him and making her jump. "And speaking of which, I want to nail some of the prelims on this tonight. Are you happy to work back?"

"Sure," she said, not happy at all.

Most of the employees had already left for Manic Monday at the local pub and while Nate hadn't given her the slightest indication he saw her as anything other than an employee—bar the fleeting butt ogling incident she'd attributed to a momentary lapse—the thought of being cocooned in his cosy office for the next few hours seemed too intimate when she'd rather keep her distance.

"Good. I'll order in dinner," he said. Chinese okay?"

She nodded, instantly transported back to that night in Singapore when they'd feasted on fried rice and other Asian delicacies before feasting on each other.

"Any preferences?"

"I'm not fussy."

Taking a peek at him from beneath her lashes as he ordered the food via an app on his phone, she wondered if he ever thought about that magical night. Though he was civil to her during work hours he'd gone cold since her first day, almost as if he'd deliberately erected a barrier she couldn't breach.

"Right, that's done," he said, placing his phone on his desk. "Let's get to it."

They worked steadily for the next half hour, with Kris making frantic annotations on her paperwork as the ideas flowed fast and furious between them. She'd worked with some of the best around the world but bouncing ideas with Nate took creativity to a whole new level and Hallie's knock on the door almost came as a welcome reprieve as Kristen's mind spun.

"Hey guys, your dinner has arrived." Hallie dumped it on the table, took one look at the stack of work in front of them, and grimaced. "I take it you won't be making it to Manic Monday?"

"Afraid not," Nate said, leaning back in his chair, clasping his hands and stretching, the simple action creating a strange flurry in Kristen's gut and earning an appreciative smile from Hallie.

"Well then, I'm off." Hallie turned her back on Nate and sent Kristen a huge wink as she headed for the door. "Don't work too hard, guys. And don't spend all night with your noses to the grindstone."

"I'm not that dedicated," Kristen mumbled, the spicy aromas from the takeout boxes making her nose twitch and her tummy rumble as Hallie closed the door, leaving her all too aware of exactly how good it was to spend all night with Nate.

"I think you are dedicated," Nate said, gesturing towards her presentation. "And your boss is suitable impressed, but why don't we take a break and dig in?"

"Sounds good to me."

She placed her pen and pad on the table and worked the kinks out of her neck, surprised to find Nate hadn't moved a muscle when she finally looked up. Instead, a slow-burning heat turned his eyes to molten chocolate as he smiled, the first time she'd seen him send her anything other than a frown for the last week.

"What?"

If his cold treatment left her flustered, it was nothing on how she felt basking in the warmth spilling from his eyes now.

"We're both very driven," he finally said, reaching for the takeout cartons and handing her chopsticks as if the loaded moment had never happened.

"Yeah, we are," she mumbled, accepting one of the boxes and opening it before shovelling Singapore noodles into her mouth with gusto.

She'd skipped lunch trying to put the final touches on her presentation and was starving. By the avaricious gleam in Nate's eye and the way he kept staring at her, it looked like she wasn't the only one, though by the surprising glint in his eyes he preferred her to the food. Yeah, right. Hunger was probably making her hallucinate.

"Good?" He'd barely touched his chilli chicken while her chopsticks were perilously close to scraping the bottom of her noodle box.

"Fabulous," she said.

"Almost as good as the meal we shared in Singapore?"

Her heart skipped a beat. Surely Mr. Professional hadn't just referred to the one night they'd vowed to ignore?

She could've taken the easy way out and opted for a nice, safe response, the type of answer he'd expect.

But where would the fun be in that?

"Nothing could be as good as that night," she said, eyeballing him.

He didn't blink.

He didn't look away.

Instead they sat there for what seemed like an eternity, the air crackling between them, bound by the same tension that had made them lose their heads that one, magical, balmy night several months ago.

"You're right," he murmured, taking a stab at a piece of chicken with his chopsticks and coming up empty considering his eyes hadn't left hers.

In that moment Kris knew no matter how cool Nate pretended to be, he hadn't forgotten what they'd shared.

"Well, we better eat up and get back to it," she said, the false brightness in her tone almost making her cringe.

But she had to do something to get them back on track, away from the touchy subject of that incredible night and how much she'd like to recreate the same magic again the longer he stared at her with fire in those hypnotic eyes.

"Right," he snapped, and in an instant the heat between them evaporated, to be replaced by Nate's cool indifference, and Kristen stifled a sigh.

After all, she'd got what she wanted. An acknowledgement that the magic they'd created in Singapore hadn't been a figment of her imagination.

Hadn't she?

Ten

"Kristen, where are we at with the casting for Travelogue?"

Kristen glared at Nate, convinced he was picking on her as the newbie on purpose. His abrupt question, combined with his condescending tone, made her want to throttle him.

"We're on schedule. The final screen tests are done and we're expecting visa clearance for the last cast member as we speak."

A tiny frown she'd grown to recognise appeared between his brows. "That's all well and good but what's the actual time frame? Are we talking days or hours here? I need direct answers, not vague platitudes."

Stiffening, Kristen twirled a pen between her fingers, refraining from stabbing it into her notebook to make a point; or better yet stabbing it into the man who had made her working life miserable for the last two weeks since she'd started.

She didn't get it.

He'd been fine on her first day, and later at Manic Monday

had been the epitome of a chivalrous gentleman waiting until she reached her car. Most guys took her confident persona as a sign she could take care of herself—and she could—but it had been nice to feel protected for that brief moment.

However, since that night he'd closed off—discounting the slight aberration during their working dinner when he'd thawed for all of two seconds—their conversations were cold and clipped, his demeanour bordering on antagonistic, and she'd had enough. Once this meeting was over she'd confront him.

"The Victorian travel department doesn't work to your schedule and they can't give me precise times. As soon as the visas come through, I assure you, you'll be the first to know."

She shouldn't have spoken to him like that, not with Alan watching their sparring with avid interest, but there was only so much she could take and Nate had crossed the line about a week ago with his surly attitude.

"Fine," Nate muttered. "Let's adjourn until we have confirmation."

If looks could kill she would've curled up her toes on the spot but she didn't flinch from his glowering glare. He could say things were fine but she knew differently and she had every intention of finding out what was going on. What had happened to his holier than thou 'we're professionals and can handle that night between us' speech he'd given on the first day? Gone as quickly as the special spark she'd imagined they'd once shared.

"Keep me posted," Alan said, gathering up his paperwork and heading for the door in record time.

Maybe her poker face needed some work because Alan shot her a concerned glance on his way out, obviously not wanting to get caught in the crossfire once she let Nate have it.

"Thanks Alan, shall do," she said, forcing a smile that faded once the door closed and she turned to face the boss.

"We're finished here," he said, sliding documents into clear plastic sleeves and shoving the lot into a box he hefted onto his hip.

"On the contrary, we're just getting started." She planted her hands on the conference table and leaned forward, fixing him with a glare that had wilted lesser men. "I want to know what's going on."

"We had a business meeting as far as I can tell," he said, placing the box on the table, his exasperation audible.

"Don't patronise me," she said, hating the tension between them, hating the fact she cared more. "You've been giving me a hard time ever since I started. I've done everything you've asked of me and more, yet you can't be civil? What's with that?"

He froze, his expression icy. "I treat you like any other employee. If you expect special treatment, forget it."

"Why would you think I'd expect special treatment?"

Though she knew and the thought sent anger spearing through her. Would he ever let her forget the mistake she'd made in Singapore?

"Look, this is getting us nowhere. I'm sorry if you think I've been too pushy or tyrannical but it's how I do business. If you don't like it maybe we need to come to another arrangement?"

"Are you threatening to fire me?" She gripped the table, her blood pressure soaring and spots dancing before her eyes. "You're unbelievable..." The words died on her lips as she swayed, the spots joined by squiggles and stars and quickly followed by darkness as she collapsed onto the table.

Nathan's blood chilled as he watched Kris slump forward in a heap, her head making a god-awful sound as it thumped on the table. He rushed forward in time to catch her before she slid to the floor, struck by two things simultaneously: how scared he was that she'd injured herself and how petrified he was by how good she felt cradled in his arms.

"What happened?" Her eyelids fluttered open and he breathed a sigh of relief, unaware he'd been holding his breath.

"You passed out," he said, brushing strands of hair off her forehead, wishing the lump of fear lodged in his throat would disappear. The longer she stared at him with uncertainty in her wide blue eyes, the larger the lump grew until he could hardly speak.

"I've never fainted in my life," she said, her brow creased as if puzzling over what had happened.

"Maybe you've been pushing yourself too hard?"

He had been, inundating her with work in a warped plan to push her away, ensuring they both stayed busy so he wouldn't be tempted to lower his professional barriers.

"I'm used to working at a hectic pace," she said, shaking her head and wincing as she reached up to feel the growing bump near her hairline. "Ouch, that must've been some knock."

"It was. Shook the building, I'd say," he deadpanned, relieved when she grinned.

"Who asked you?" Her rueful smile faded as her fingers connected with the bump and his heart clenched with the fragile glint in her eyes.

"Here, let me check it out."

Expecting her to protest, she surprised him by lowering her hand and closing her eyes as his fingertips skimmed the bump on her forehead and beyond, using gentle pressure to explore her scalp for further damage, relieved he didn't find any.

Though his relief was short-lived as he registered how wonderful it felt to be running his fingers through her hair, just like he had that night he'd been trying so damn hard to forget.

After pulling his hand back as if scalded, he raised her to a sitting position, needing to get her out of his arms before he did something crazy, like kiss her bump better and follow up with a kiss on her lips to make him feel better.

"You should see a doctor, get yourself checked out," he said, propping her against a chair and reaching for a glass of water from the table and handing it to her.

"I hate going to doctors," she said, taking a gingerly sip before closing her eyes tight again, pain contorting her face.

His heart flipped with concern. "What's wrong?"

"I think I'm going to be sick."

"Hell," he muttered, casting a frantic glance around the room for something to act as a sick bag and coming up empty.

"Just give me a second, it might pass," she said, taking slow, deep breaths and looking paler by the minute.

Hating the helplessness rendering him useless, he grabbed one of the clear plastic sleeves containing the month's projection figures and tipped them out in a hurry. It would do as a sick bag at a pinch.

Her eyes snapped open and she fixed him with an accusatory glare. "Don't think this means we finished our conversation. As soon as I'm feeling better you're going to face the music, mister."

He smiled, relieved to see some of the familiar fire return to her eyes, and amused she'd think of chewing him out at a time like this.

"Duly warned," he said, taking hold of her arm. "Think you can stand? I'll help you up then grab my phone so you can call your doc."

"I don't think—"

"Don't think, just call. You need a check up, as I won't

stand for one of my prized employees collapsing on me for no reason."

Rather than arguing as he expected, she accepted his assistance and he got her onto a chair without further drama, though he should've known she wouldn't stay silent for long.

"If this is how you treat prized employees I'd hate to see how you treat the ones you don't value."

Sliding his phone out of the pocket of his jacket draped over the back of his chair, he said, "Hey, didn't I stop you from falling on the floor in an undignified heap?"

She waved away his response, the colour returning to her cheeks. "Not that, the way you've been carrying on the last two weeks."

"We'll talk about that later," he said, handing her the phone. "Now, search for your doc's number if you don't know it off by heart. I'm not letting you out of my sight until you're in a taxi and on the way to see him or her."

"I don't have a doctor in Melbourne," she said, thrusting out her bottom lip in a delightful pout that matched her sulky tone.

"Then you can see mine. Doc Rubin is one of the best," he said, pulling up his contacts and stabbing at the number, fixing her with a glare that brooked no argument.

"I'm feeling fine now. It was probably the result of long hours and snatched meals."

"Something tells me you've always worked like that yet you said you haven't fainted before?"

He waited while the doc's receptionist put him on hold, hoping he wasn't over-reacting. Maybe she was right and this was a one-off? However, seeing her so helpless, lying there with her eyes closed, and cradling her limp body, had resurrected stark memories of holding Julia in a similar way. He'd been too late to save her and he'd be damned if he dismissed

Kris's fainting spell out of hand when it could indicate something more serious than overwork.

"You're being awfully bossy," she muttered, her arms crossed over her chest in an action he'd come to associate with her stubbornness several times during meetings over the last few weeks.

"Funny, considering I'm your boss."

He held up his hand as the receptionist came on the phone and he took the first available appointment, which happened to be in half an hour courtesy of a cancellation.

Thanking the receptionist, he disconnected. "Right. We're all set. Let's go."

"You're not coming with me."

Her horrified glare told him exactly what she thought of the idea of his accompanying her and he paused, struck by how inappropriate it might look for the boss to be seen mollycoddling an employee.

She's more than that and you know it.

Ignoring his annoying inner voice, he said, "Actually, I was thinking Hallie could ride with you." He held up his hand as she opened her mouth to protest. "Don't even think about arguing. You can't be alone in case you collapse again so Hallie is accompanying you, okay?"

"Okay," she said, her meek tone telling him exactly how scared she was but trying to hide it. "But this doctor better be good."

Hiding a triumphant grin, he said, "You'll be in good hands with Doc Rubin. And make sure you head home straight from the surgery. I don't want to see you back here, got it?"

"Is that ever?"

He ignored her jibe in reference to their earlier conversation, aware he'd have to do some fast talking once she was better. Anything rather than tell her the truth.

"I'll call you later to see how you feel," he said, offering her a hand to help her up from the chair, which she ignored now she had some strength back.

He should've known her dependence wouldn't last long. She'd never accept a helping hand from him unless desperate.

"Do you need assistance to the front door of the building?"

"I'm fine." She stopped short of rolling her eyes and he grinned, holding his hands up in surrender. "Don't think this lets you off the hook. I'll be back to bust your butt faster than you can say 'that's a wrap.'"

"I look forward to it," he said, thinking that for a woman who presented a stern front she had a delightful sense of humour and he much preferred being on the receiving end of a funny barb than the killer glare she did all too well.

Then again, he'd done such a good job of alienating her, maybe busting his butt wasn't a joke?

Keeping her at arms length was proving to be more difficult than he'd anticipated.

Perhaps he had to try harder.

Eleven

"You're pregnant."

Kristen stared in horror at Doctor Rubin, who was a dead ringer for Santa Claus. Ironic, considering she'd never believed in the jolly fat guy, especially as he never brought her what she wanted: a family. No surprise his lookalike delivered shocking news she didn't believe too.

"There has to be some kind of mistake," she said, folding her arms and fixing him with a withering stare.

The doctor shook his head, a kindly smile on his rotund face. "No mistake, Miss Lewis. Can you tell me the date of your last period so I can calculate your due date?"

Right then, the first flicker of doubt set in. Last period... When had that been? She'd attributed her lateness to changing time zones, the move to Melbourne and the stress of a new job. It wouldn't be the first time she'd missed periods at a tough time in her life.

Never in her wildest dreams—or nightmares—had she considered she could be pregnant.

Struggling to remember, she said, "Over twelve weeks ago? I'd have to check my diary for the exact date."

"We can go into that later but right now let me give you a rough estimate."

While the doctor twirled a cardboard circle peppered with numbers, she sank into the chair and furiously tried to marshal her thoughts.

She couldn't be pregnant.

She didn't know the first thing about being a mother let alone caring for a child.

She didn't even like kids.

How on earth had this happened?

An icy shiver spread cold, clammy fingers through her body. She hadn't slept with anyone apart from Nate, which meant...

"Your due date is December first."

She squeezed her eyes shut and shook her head from side to side in a futile attempt to vanquish the logical explanation as to who the father of the baby was. The only explanation.

"I hate to state the obvious but this pregnancy is unexpected?"

Her eyes snapped open and her shocked gaze met the doctor's understanding eyes, hating the anger bubbling within her at the futility of her situation. A baby had never been in her grand plan. She had a successful career and an orderly; she didn't need the complication of a child and all the responsibility he or she entailed.

Damn it, they'd used protection. How could this happen?

Rubbing a hand across her eyes, she tried to erase the vivid image that flashed across her mind in response to that particular question.

"We can discuss options," Doctor Rubin said, his voice devoid of emotion or judgement.

She didn't want to discuss options. She wanted to run screaming from his office, head home, dive under her duvet and hide away from the truth: pregnant, to her boss.

Taking a deep breath, she slid a protective hand over her flat belly. She needed time to think, time to absorb the shock, time to figure out what she wanted to do, though in reality she knew it would take a lifetime to get used to the idea of her as a mother—and Nate as her child's father.

Lifting her chin, she met the doctor's concerned stare. "That won't be necessary."

"Good. In that case let's discuss obstetricians. You'll need to have your first review and ultrasound ASAP as you're already past twelve weeks."

"Fine," she said, knowing it wasn't.

Making the decision to be a mother was one thing, facing up to specialists and ultrasounds and goodness knows what another. Apart from knowing next to nothing about kids, she didn't have the faintest idea what pregnancy entailed—apart from the obvious like nausea and swollen ankles and a belly the size of a basketball. She had no friends to ask and the thought of going through this alone hit hard.

Though there was Nate...

Nate, who could barely bring himself to look at her these days let alone acknowledge the one night he'd made clear meant nothing to him had resulted in a baby.

How could she tell him something like this? How would he react? What a mess.

"Right. Here's a list of obstetricians and the multi-vitamins I recommend you commence immediately. Any other questions?"

Kristen stared at the doctor. Was he crazy? She had a heap of them starting with 'how bad will the labour be?' and ending with 'how will I care for a baby?'

However, she swallowed her questions and shook her head. If she spent one more minute in this doctor's office with his twinkly eyes and benevolent smile she'd start blubbering and never stop.

"No, I'm right for now. Thanks for your help." She stood, pressing the information he'd given her to her chest like a shield, and headed for the door.

"Miss Lewis?"

She paused and turned back. "Yes?"

"Congratulations. Bringing a baby into this world is a truly wonderful experience."

Easy for him to say. He was a man.

She managed a grim smile that must've come out a grimace and tore out of the room, stuffing the information into her handbag, desperately craving fresh air and a reality check.

"Hey, wait up," Hallie called out from the waiting room and Kristen forced her feet to stop.

She needed time to compute what the doctor had told her and if her overzealous friend got wind of her predicament the news would travel around RX with the speed of a film on fast forward.

"What's wrong?" Hallie touched her arm. "Are you all right?"

Kristen nodded, knowing nothing would ever be right again. "I've got some virus."

Hallie's eyes narrowed as if she didn't believe a word of it. "Why were you tearing out of here like a bat out of hell?"

"Needed fresh air." Kristen fanned her face and faked a slight stagger, feeling guilty when Hallie made a 'be right back' sign at the medical receptionist and hauled her outside before she collapsed.

Taking in deep breaths and feeling like the worst kind of fraud for deceiving the closest person she had to calling a friend, Kristen braced herself against a brick wall.

"Must be some virus to make you faint," Hallie said, her head cocked to one side like a curious sparrow.

"Mmm," Kristen mumbled noncommittally, wondering when she legally had to inform RX about her condition.

Her condition.

She hated pregnancy labelled that way, like it was an illness and not a natural part of life. The women she'd worked with had been having babies, not suffering from some debilitating sickness, yet colleagues had blamed the slightest thing—from a missed meeting to a late memo—on their 'condition.'

She hadn't fought it back then, not deeming it relevant, but boy did she have a different outlook now. The first person to label her with a *condition* would get slugged. Though that could be the hormones kicking in and making her want to slug anybody, including the infuriating guy who'd got her into this predicament in the first place.

"Ready to go back inside? I'm sure that beady-eyed woman thought we were running out of there without paying. Typical receptionist." Hallie rolled her eyes and Kristen laughed for the first time in hours.

Hopefully, she could be that self-deprecating when the time came for her to face the inevitable sly comments about her pregnancy.

Grateful for Hallie's presence, she reached out and squeezed her hand. "Thanks for being here. You've done nothing but make me feel welcome since I started at RX and I really appreciate it."

Hallie blushed. "No worries. For an uptight exec, you're okay."

"Enough with the compliments." Kristen returned her smile. "Can you do me a favour?"

"Sure."

"Let Nathan know I'm fine? I think he kind of freaked out when I fainted in that meeting and said he'd call me later, but I just want to head home and go to bed."

"No worries, I'll tell him," Hallie said, bristling like a

protective mom before continuing. "He's a great boss, isn't he? Not many big-wigs would take an interest in their employees like he does."

Kristen stilled. Was Hallie fishing for info? Had she sensed a past connection between Nate and her?

"I've worked with worse," she said, keeping her voice devoid of emotion, hoping to nip Hallie's possible fishing expedition in the bud. "Now, let me pay this bill, organise taxis for us and head home. I'm beat."

"Okay."

Hallie didn't push the issue and Kristen attributed her comments to run of the mill frank statements the receptionist was famous for. Hallie thought the boss was great? Well, Kristen would soon find out if that were true once Nate heard that his newest exec was pregnant.

More importantly, that he was the father.

"Though I'll share the taxi to your place then head home from there." Kristen opened her mouth to argue but Hallie held up a hand. "It's not open for debate. Besides, this may be the only chance I ever get to boss you around."

Hallie winked and in a small way Kristen was happy to have the company home. Chatting to Hallie might keep her mind off her predicament—for all of two seconds.

She paid the bill and called a cab, her head spinning the entire time and thankfully, Hallie kept up a steady stream of conversation until they reached her place. However, as soon as she laid eyes on her terrace house, a thousand doubts plagued her: could she bring up a child in a place like this? Was it too small? What about the steep stairs? And the split level lounge? And her totally impractical furniture?

"Kris, are you okay?" Hallie covered her hand with hers and with that small, caring gesture Kristen burst into tears.

Not dainty tears but huge drops that poured down her

cheeks and plopped onto her cream linen skirt, accompanied by sobbing, hiccups, the works.

"I'll take it from here," Hallie said, thrusting the fare at a bemused taxi driver and assisting her out of the taxi like an invalid.

"I'm sorry," Kristen murmured, trying to stem the tears, only to find they flowed faster as she unlocked her front door and stumbled into the hallway.

"Hey, don't apologise. Viruses can make us do strange things." By the dubious look on Hallie's face, she didn't believe the virus story for a second. "Now sit and I'll get you something to drink. What would you like?"

"Water please. Kitchen's through there."

"I'll find my way around," Hallie said, casting her a concerned glance before hurrying away, giving Kristen valuable time to regain control.

She never cried. Ever. She'd had plenty of opportunity in the past thanks to her upbringing but tears were seen as a sign of weakness by bullies and she'd soon learned to never give them an inkling of her emotions. Now, it looked like the floodgates had opened and wouldn't stop in a hurry.

"Here you go." Hallie thrust a tall glass of water into her hand and sat on the couch next to her, waiting until she'd drained most of it and her tears had subsided before speaking. "You know I'm your friend, right?"

Kristen nodded, surprised to find she did consider Hallie a friend. They'd bonded over a few coffees at work and she'd almost blurted the sorry tale about Nate's cold treatment several times but had stopped at the last minute, aware loose lips sunk exec producer's ships. However, if ever she needed a friend, now was it.

"In that case, why don't you tell me what's really going on?"

Kristen opened her mouth to fob Hallie off, to repeat the

virus story, to give her any number of false platitudes. Instead, "I'm pregnant," popped out.

Hallie's eyes widened to the size of dinner plates. "You're preggers? For real?"

"Yeah, it's real," Kristen said, rubbing her flat belly in a reflex action, finding it almost impossible to equate herself—the ultimate career girl—becoming a mother. "The doc just told me. I had no idea."

"Wow." Hallie collapsed back against the cushions, her stunned expression soon replaced by the cheeky grin Kristen had grown accustomed to. "Who's the father? Anyone I know?"

Hallie's exaggerated, conspiratorial wink should've made Kristen laugh. Instead, dread shot through her at the thought of anyone at work finding out Nate was the father before he did.

Forcing a nonchalant tone, Kristen said, "No."

Not a lie exactly. The Nate she'd known for that one brief magical night in Singapore was nothing like the Nathan Boyd that Hallie knew.

"So you're doing this on your own? That's pretty brave."

"Actually, I have no idea what I'm going to do."

Hallie's grin faded. "You're going to keep it, right?"

"Uh-huh."

Kristen's tentative response encapsulated her doubts. She'd never contemplate any other outcome than going through with this pregnancy, but not wanting this baby had nothing to do with her lifestyle or job and everything to do with the gut-wrenching fear gnawing at her since childhood, the soul-destroying terror she'd never be a good mother because she'd never had one herself.

Being shunted from foster home to foster home had fuelled her fear, where the women so casually labelled mothers wouldn't know the first thing about caring or nurturing a child. Instead, their focus had been strictly on the dollars allocated from the government for the care of parentless kids like her and she'd grown to hate their callous indifference.

"You don't sound convinced?"

Straightening, Kristen said, "I'm having this baby."

She may not have the foggiest idea how to be a good parent but she knew she could do a better job than the poor excuses that had raised her.

"Fabulous." Hallie clapped her hands like an excited child. "I can be a surrogate aunt. Though I still think you're super brave to be doing this alone."

Kristen shrugged, strangely uncomfortable with admiration she didn't deserve. "Not really. There are loads of single parents out there. I'm just adding to the statistics."

"Yeah, but a baby? Man, is that going to cramp your style." Hallie's eyes sparkled as she sent a pointed look at her fitted skirt and matching jacket. "Especially your clothes style. Mind if you throw a few casts-offs my way? Your outfits are to die for."

Kristen chuckled. Nothing fazed Hallie, even an unexpected pregnancy, and she hoped Nate took the news as well.

"I hate to tell you but I won't be the size of a house for long. I plan on getting back into my clothes one day."

"Too bad." Hallie smiled and smothered her in a hug. "Actually, this is cool. It's the best news I've heard in ages. Congrats, Kris. You're going to be a great mum."

"Thanks," Kristen mumbled, disengaging from Hallie's bear hug to gulp the rest of her water to dislodge the lump of emotion stuck in throat, fervently hoping the tears wouldn't start again.

"You know you can count on me, right?"

Kristen nodded and made a frantic grab for a tissue out of her handbag, dabbing at her eyes before she turned on the waterworks again. "Stop trying to make me cry." She sniffled, while Hallie grinned and slid an arm around her shoulders.

"Okay. I'll stop. And by the way, don't worry. Your secret's safe with me."

"It better be. I haven't had a chance to tell Nathan yet and apply for leave."

Hallie gave her a comforting squeeze. "The boss will be fine about it. He'll hire a maternity leave replacement for your position and you'll be back before you can say 'poopy nappy.'"

"I hope you're right," Kristen said, managing a watery smile.

She had no qualms about Nate accepting the news of her impending motherhood and granting her maternity leave.

It was the news that he was the father of her baby she had her concerns about.

"What about the dad? Are you going to tell him?"

Her stomach somersaulted. "I hadn't thought that far ahead."

"You know it's the right thing to do?"

Hallie's astute stare made Kristen squirm and she shuffled back on the couch, picked up a cushion, and hugged it to her tummy.

"Right?" Hallie prompted.

"I've barely absorbed the news myself," Kristen said, knowing that no amount of time would make this decision any easier.

"Well, if you don't, I think you're selfish." Hallie flopped back and folded her arms, her mouth a surprising sulky pout.

"Tell me what you really think," Kristen muttered, hugging the cushion tighter.

A small part of her agreed with Hallie but this was Nate they were talking about. The same Nate who had erased that amazing night from his memory banks, the same Nate who had given her the cold shoulder for the last fortnight, the same Nate who was her boss.

Could she really tell him the truth?

Hallie frowned. "Every parent has a right to know if they have a child. One of my closest friend's would've given anything to know her dad but her mum always said he was dead. Well, guess what? Turned out her dad was living around the corner the entire time and when my friend turned up on his doorstep twenty years later, he was ecstatic. Mad as hell at my friend's mum for cheating him out of playing a part in her life all those years but really chuffed he had a kid. So unless your baby's father is an axe murderer, which I seriously doubt, you should tell him. It's the right thing to do."

Kristen had never seen Hallie so serious. Joking around, teasing, flippant, yeah. But delivering a stern lecture? No.

"You're probably right but I want some time to think this through, okay?"

Hallie deflated and her trademark smile returned. "Okay. But if you don't you know I'll be on your case, right?"

"I know." Kristen rolled her eyes, knowing she was lucky to have a friend like Hallie to confide in, especially considering they'd only known each other a few weeks.

"You've got some thinking to do so I'll leave you to it. Call me if you need anything?"

"Shall do." Kristen showed Hallie to the door and gave her an impulsive hug before realising she didn't have any transport home. "Hey, come back inside and I'll call a cab."

"Don't worry about it. I'll catch a tram. It'll take me ten minutes to get home, max."

"Sure?"

Hallie gave her a gentle shove back through the door. "Go. Sit down. Think."

"Okay, okay." Kristen held up her hands in surrender,

smiling as Hallie bounced down the path and waved until she rounded the street corner.

However, her smile faded as she closed the door and silence descended. She had a lot of thinking to do but did that necessarily mean she'd come up with the right answer?

Twelve

Nate braced as Kris's front door creaked open and her face appeared through the crack, a deep frown marring her brow.

He shouldn't have done a drop-in without letting her know first but he'd been so concerned he couldn't concentrate at work. Hallie's half-hearted reassurance about some vague virus Kris had didn't help and he'd had to see for himself she was okay.

"Hi, how are you feeling?"

"Better." She opened the door a fraction further, the frown intensifying as she fiddled with a chain. "What are you doing here?"

"Sorry to drop by unannounced but I was worried about you."

"You don't need to be, I'm fine."

The chain clattered against the door frame but she didn't invite him in. Instead, she hid behind the door, only her head visible.

"Hallie said it's some kind of virus?"

"That's right."

Her lips compressed into a thin line and she glared at him like Doc Rubin had diagnosed her with a terminal illness rather than a transient one. So much for being concerned. He was floundering way out of his depth and had made a major mistake dropping by.

"I'm glad you're okay. If you need more time off work, take it."

"I'll be in first thing in the morning," she said, her tone softening as she opened the door wider. "Look, you may as well come in now you're here. I'm not dressed to receive visitors and you took me by surprise showing up out of the blue like this."

"You sure? I don't want to impose."

Her raised eyebrow told him he already had. "You better come in before I change my mind and slam the door in your face."

"Put like that, how can I refuse?"

He stepped into the hallway, quickly averting his gaze when he caught sight of the long, silky purple kimono draping the gorgeous body he remembered all too well.

"The lounge is through there. Make yourself comfortable while I get dressed."

He opened his mouth to protest and snapped it shut again. He didn't want her changing, especially if she was comfortable, but having to sit across from her dressed in that sexy robe, wondering if she was naked beneath it, would make him extremely uncomfortable.

She padded up the stairs, her bare feet softly thudding against the worn boards and he watched her for a moment, admiring the gentle swish of silk around her ankles and the way the material draped her butt, before heading for the lounge room and not up the stairs like he wanted to.

This was a bad idea.

If seeing her in those sexy power-suits on a daily basis was bad enough, that flowing kimono set his mind on tangents he shouldn't be contemplating.

Stepping into the lounge room, he did another double-take. The outside of the quaint terrace house had a homely feel, with its cream rendering and bottle green fretwork, but this room quickly dispelled that impression with its stark modernistic furniture, all sleek lines and devoid of colour. Beige walls, beige suede sofas, and a large beige rug covering the pale floorboards, without a splash of contrasting colour in sight.

Another noticeable absent feature was photos. She'd told him she didn't have much family apart from two sisters but it looked like they didn't rank highly on her scale of personal importance if their absence in photographic memories was any indication. He didn't have many lying around any more either but that was because of the painful memories every time he caught an unexpected glimpse of Julia's smile or the characteristic sparkle in her eyes he'd loved since high school.

He did a slow three-sixty, chilled by the lifeless ambience of the room. Kris was a vibrant, outgoing woman. What was she doing living in a place like this? A place built for families and love and warmth on the outside yet cold and indifferent on the inside? What did that say about the woman he thought he knew?

"Would you like something to drink?"

He spun around, forcing a smile to hide his discomfort. "I'm fine, thanks."

She hovered in the doorway, her blue eyes stark in her pale face, highlighted by the bright red of her T-shirt worn loose over dark denim jeans.

He was used to dealing with a super confidant woman strutting around the office. This waif-like Kris had him wanting to do all sorts of uncharacteristic things like cradle her close and stroke her tousled blonde hair.

"Why don't you tell me why you're really here?"

She leaned against the doorjamb, hands thrust into the pockets of her jeans, her feet bare, and the fire-engine red of her painted toenails a perfect match for her T shirt. Her pallor should've highlighted her vulnerability. However, nothing could dim the intelligence behind her direct stare and he knew she'd settle for nothing less than the truth.

"Fine, but only if you sit down. You're making me nervous."

Quirking a brow, she padded across the room and chose the armchair furthest from him. "Okay, start talking."

Rather than curling up and tucking her feet under like most people would in their own home, she perched on the edge of the chair as if ready for flight.

"My main reason for dropping by was to check on you, but there's something else."

"I gathered that."

She didn't encourage him or set him at ease, her rigid posture indicative of the hands-off approach she'd adopted with him. Not that he could blame her considering he'd been doing the same.

Sitting opposite, he leaned back on a sofa that felt as stiff as it looked. "I owe you an apology."

"Go on."

He couldn't read her blank expression but the banked fire in her eyes spoke volumes: she intended to roast him over his behaviour and then make him sweat to be forgiven.

"I've been pushing you hard these last few weeks, much harder than anyone else at the station. And I'm having one hell of a guilt attack about the role all the extra work I've hefted on you might've played in you coming down with this bug."

For the first time since he'd arrived, a crooked smile lit her face. "Save your guilt. Work had nothing to do with how I'm feeling."

He paused, staggered by how one, small, barely-there smile could pack such a powerful punch, slamming into him with the precise hook of a prize fighter.

"Nice of you to let me off so easily but viruses tend to strike when you're run down and I've been pushing you hard. Why don't you take the rest of the week off, rest up, and come back next Monday?"

She shook her head, the smile vanishing in an instant, replaced by the stubborn compression of lips he'd come to associate with his star executive producer. He'd seen a similar mutinous expression every time he'd brought up an idea at work she didn't agree with, every time he questioned her rationale.

"Thanks, but I'm fine. I'll be there bright and early tomorrow. If you ever let me get some sleep, that is."

She cast a pointed look at her watch and he stood, wishing he could bridge the yawning gap between them. He didn't want to get too close but he'd be damned if they continued in this cold manner.

"I miss the easy going rapport we had in Singapore," he said, holding out his hand to help her up, knowing he shouldn't have brought up the night they'd sworn to forget but unable to stop. He needed to do something to shock her out of the casual indifference shrouding her like armour.

He expected her to ignore his outstretched hand but yet again she surprised him, placing her hand in his and allowing him to pull her to her feet.

"I do too," she said, so softly he had to lean forward to catch her words, which would've been fine if it hadn't brought him scant inches away from her lush mouth and close enough to smell her faint rose essence, as subtle and enticing as a stroll through a garden on a warm summer's day.

She stared at him, her blue eyes wide with uncertainty, and his heart clenched at the vulnerability behind the tough girl exterior. For all her bravado, Kris called to him on a deeper level and if he wasn't careful he'd find himself sucked into a vortex of emotion he didn't want.

"Friends?" He squeezed her hand, wishing he could raise it to his lips and kiss it, wishing he could hold it forever.

But he wasn't a forever type of guy, not any more.

The vulnerability in her eyes quickly faded, replaced by her usual tough veneer, and she pulled her hand out of his. "Friends it is."

She headed for the hallway and he had no option but to follow, trailing after her like some teenager with a crush.

"Remember, if you need extra time off—"

"See you tomorrow," she said, holding open the door and scuffing her foot impatiently on the floor.

"Right-o." He brushed past her, knowing his visit hadn't achieved much more than make a start in broaching the yawning gap between them.

She hadn't bought his faux apology. He'd wanted to apologise for pushing her away, for treating her like a stranger rather than a woman who had woken him out of a three year stupor, but he'd baulked at the last minute, covering it up by referring to work.

So he wasn't ready to bare his soul? He'd reached out to her, hadn't he? By referring to their night of passion and the camaraderie they'd shared he'd admitted he hadn't forgotten it. Nor did he want to and in finally broaching the subject maybe he could move beyond this obsession for the woman standing in front of him, looking ready to boot him down the front path.

"Was there something else?"

"Actually, there was." He paused, searching for the right words, knowing he had to make up for the way he'd treated her. "You're a smart woman. I guess you've realised I haven't only been pushing you hard, I've been behaving like a bastard as well."

"I wouldn't put it that strongly," she said, the corners of her mouth twitching and drawing his attention to the fullness of her lips, those same lips that had prompted him to lose his mind one balmy night in Singapore.

"It's true and we both know it. I'd just like to say it's going to stop."

Her lips curved into a full-fledged grin, alleviating some of the tired lines tugging her mouth. "About time. Though if I'd known the results a quick-fire faint would produce, I would've tried it last week."

He grimaced. "Was I really that bad?"

"Worse." Shadows darkened her eyes, her frailty urging him to sweep her into his arms and never let go.

"I'm sorry," he murmured, reaching out to cup her cheek, unable to stop himself from touching her, from reassuring her he'd be doing things differently from now on.

"No worries," she said, her wide-eyed blue gaze locked on his as she moved her cheek an infinitesimal millimetre and leaned into his hand.

Powerless to resist the urge he'd had since he first laid eyes on her tonight, he broached the gap between them, slid his hand around to cradle her head and lowered his mouth to hers.

She sighed as his lips grazed hers, soft and coaxing, in the barest of kisses. However, he should've known a gentle kiss wouldn't be enough, not nearly enough, with this incredible woman and the moment she angled her head slightly was the moment he lost it.

His arms slid around her and pulled her flush against him, relishing their perfect fit as his mouth recaptured hers, deepening the kiss until he could barely breathe for wanting her.

Desire slammed through him, his mind and common

sense in meltdown as he kissed her with all the pent-up passion that had been steadily building since she'd re-entered his life a few weeks ago. A crazy, fiery, no-holds-barred kiss sending his libido into orbit and their working relationship up in flames.

After what seemed like an eternity, Kris braced her hands on his chest and eased him away, her breathing ragged and her eyes flashing fire.

"That wasn't very professional," she said, her voice deliberately cool and in stark contrast to her flushed cheeks.

"No, I guess not."

Unable to keep a satisfied grin off his face, he turned away from her confused stare and strode down the concrete path away from temptation.

Thirteen

"It's fantastic." Kristen turned to Nate and struggled not to fling her arms around him as her gaze reluctantly left the TV screen and focussed on the man who had backed her one hundred percent on this exciting project.

Nate tried a mock frown and failed, his answering grin setting her heart thudding. "Hmm...I'm not sure. Could do with a bit of work?"

"Are you serious?" She stood and stalked across the conference room to fill a cup with water and wondering when she'd last felt this energised and on top of things.

"No, I'm not serious." He chuckled and she swivelled to face him, hand on hip.

She jabbed her finger in his direction. "Joke all you like but we both know what we've just seen is going to take the Australian broadcasting industry by storm."

"That's what I like to see. Confidence."

He joined her at the water cooler, invading her personal space with his presence, standing so close her body warmed from the heat radiating off his and she took a subtle step back, needing to re-establish some distance between them.

Exuberance over success in the workplace was one thing; jumping her boss because she couldn't get the memory of that unexpected, scintillating kiss on her doorstep a week ago out of her mind, another.

"Tell me it's not the best travel show you've ever seen."

He drained his water and lobbed the paper cup in the trash before turning to face her, the excitement in his eyes a dead giveaway before he responded. "Honestly? It's some of the best work I've ever seen. You've done an incredible job, Kris."

He touched her arm, an all-too-brief squeeze designed to convey his pleasure in her work, but predictably, her pulse raced and her imagination took flight, resurrecting the many ways he'd touched her all those months ago on that one special night.

"Thanks." She headed back to the table and started gathering up her portfolio, needing to escape. In her current buoyant mood, spending one second longer with Nate could prove disastrous. Along with her fertile imagination, she had a distinct case of pregnancy hormones sending her libido crazy, and with a sexy guy like Nate around it was becoming increasingly harder to think of him in boss terms only.

"You know this means I'm going to expect a high standard from you all the time, right?"

She jumped, his voice coming from way too close over her right shoulder, and she shovelled documents faster. "No problems. At least I know if I keep producing work of this calibre you'll be nice to me."

Oops. She hadn't meant to say the last bit even if she thought it was the truth. Ever since that unexpected kiss he'd changed for the better in the workplace and they'd grown closer, developing a strong working bond fast moving towards friendship. She'd attributed his change to her performance but maybe there was something more behind the turnaround?

"I've already apologised for my earlier behaviour," he said, reaching out and taking hold of her arms before slowly turning her around to face him.

Determined not to let him see how he affected her, she tilted her chin up and hoped her expression wouldn't give away her turbulent emotions: fear he'd revert back to being cold, fear of this new and improved Nate, but most of all fear of how easily she could fall for him given half a chance.

"I know, I remember." How could she forget? She'd been ready to deck him that night on her doorstep, then he'd kissed her senseless, undermining all her defences with one, swift, scorching lip-lock.

Something akin to desire flickered in his eyes before he dropped his hands and turned away. "Good. In that case, you know I meant what I said. That's all in the past. We're a great team and I intend for us to have a long and profitable relationship."

His matter of fact tone snapped her out of the sensual fog enveloping her brain as she stilled her hands before they could rub the exact spots he'd touched her a moment ago.

Nate was her boss. She was his star employee.

They had a 'long *profitable* relationship' ahead of them.

That's all she was to him, a great worker, all she'd ever be, and no matter how much she analysed that kiss, it had been an aberration, a spur of the moment apology from a guy feeling bad about how he'd treated her.

"Right. See you tomorrow," she said, shrugging into her jacket, the tight fit reminding her of something else that would potentially bind them in a relationship, though this time it would have nothing to do with work.

She still hadn't made up her mind about telling Nate about the baby, though the closer they grew, albeit at work, she knew the time was fast approaching when she'd need to make a decision one way or the other.

"I'm really thrilled this is working out, Kris."

He glanced at her, an inscrutable expression in his dark chocolate eyes, and for a moment an irrational spark of hope flared to life that maybe, just maybe, he was referring to something other than work.

"Me too."

Forcing a cheery smile, she waved and walked away, silently praying he had no idea of the giant size crush she'd developed.

"Wow." Kristen stared at the big, flat screen while the doctor moved a detector over her stomach, skidding through the cold gel as he moved it every which way, showing her in startling clarity she was pregnant.

"The bub is a perfect size for sixteen weeks," the doctor said, whose name she'd forgotten the instant she stepped into the room, her scared gaze riveted to the monitors and screens crowding the single bed in a make-shift cubicle in his office. "I'll take a few more measurements and we'll be done here."

She nodded, barely aware of anything but the tiny baby on the screen, its knees tucked up to its chest, cosy and secure without a care in the world, while her heart raced and her palms grew damp with the enormity of what she was doing.

That little defenceless baby was hers, from its ten tiny, perfectly formed fingers to its ten miniature toes. Tears stung her eyes and she blinked rapidly, unwilling to blubber in front of a stranger. Time enough for that at the birth.

As her gaze stayed riveted to the screen, the baby's hand moved towards its face as if waving, and Kristen's heart clenched with a surge of instinctual love. In that moment, this pregnancy hit her in a tidal wave of emotion, leaving her breathless with joy, fear and anticipation.

"Almost there," the doctor said, taking snapshots of the

baby by hitting a few keys on the elaborate keyboard linked to the monitor.

She wanted to say 'take all the time in the world' because for this one significant moment in time, she realised something. Coming face to face with her baby, seeing the hard evidence she was carrying a real, live person inside of her, hammered home the enormity of the situation.

She hadn't created this tiny miracle all by herself and as much as she'd prevaricated over the dilemma of whether to tell Nate or not, seeing the evidence of the life they'd created left her with no choice.

She had to tell him.

It was the right thing to do.

Though now she'd made the decision, her stomach roiled at the thought. Since the night he'd dropped by her place a fortnight ago, they'd forged a strong working relationship. He'd released whatever hang-up he'd had the first two weeks and they'd bonded, becoming closer than she dared hope considering their capricious start. Not that they were best buddies but it was nice to consider the boss a friend rather than an enemy.

How friendly would he be when she dumped her pregnancy surprise on him?

Most guys would run a mile. Then again, Nate wasn't most guys. For a CEO who owned half of Australia's entertainment interests he didn't have a mean bone in his body, and though he hadn't shaken the inherent sadness he smiled most days, a smile that lit up her world if she was completely honest.

"All done." The doctor handed her a bunch of paper towels to wipe the gel off her tummy and when she'd finished, he gave her a small picture. "Here. One for your album."

Grinning like an idiot, she traced the baby's outline with a fingertip, unprepared for the surge of fierce, intense love arrowing through her body and lodging directly in her heart.

Though she didn't have a clue about parenting she'd be the best mother if it killed her. She'd buy countless books, take parenting classes, do whatever it took to ensure her baby had the best mom in the world.

"Thanks," she murmured, raising tear-filled eyes to see the young doctor smiling at her.

"Really hits home right about now, huh?"

She nodded, clutching the small photo so hard it creased.

"Make sure you schedule another ultrasound for twenty weeks on your way out," he said, helping her down from the table. "I'll see you then."

"Okay. Thanks."

After placing the photo on the bed, Kristen zipped up her pants and slipped her stockinged feet into stiletto pumps, her gaze never leaving the first picture of her child. *Their* child. Hers and Nate's.

Sighing, she picked up the picture and slid it into her handbag. Nate deserved to know no matter how overprotective she might feel towards her unborn baby. Whether he wanted anything to do with the baby or not, it should be his decision to make, not hers.

This baby was real.

This baby was theirs.

It was time to give Nate the news. This wasn't only about her and a good mother always put their child's needs first.

Starting now.

Fourteen

Kristen opened the door, her breath catching as she caught sight of Nate standing on her doorstep wearing dark denim, a navy T-shirt, and a smile. The guy was seriously gorgeous and she could easily fall for him given half a chance. But that was out of the question. She had a baby to care for, a life to build for them, and her needs would come a far second to that of her child.

"These are for you." He handed her five large blocks of Swiss chocolate with the gooiest, fudge caramel centres, her favourite, and she welcomed him in.

"How did you know?"

"I've seen you devouring the odd block or two at your desk."

The odd block or two? She'd bought out the local chocolatier with her intense cravings for the creamy smooth chocolate that melted on her tongue. So her baby would have a sweet tooth? If that was the worst trait he or she inherited from her, she'd be lucky.

"Have you been spying on me?"

He grinned. "Of course. I always keep an eye on my best executive producers. Jack Bane has nothing on me."

"You could give Jack a run for his money," she said, ushering him into the cosy dining room set for two and handing him a bottle opener. "In the success stakes of course."

By his cocky smile he knew exactly how she was comparing him to the channel's hottest star who carried a lucrative spy series by his popularity alone; in the sexy stakes. Her cover-up for her gaffe had been pathetic at best.

She bustled about the table, handing him the wine to uncork while she topped up her glass with sparkling mineral water.

"Wine?"

"No thanks," she said, the fumes sending a wave of nausea crashing over her.

She hadn't been too bad with morning sickness but around six in the evening her hormones surged and the faintest smell had her running for the loo.

Indicating he take a seat, she slid into the chair opposite. "I'm not having wine, though I thought you might like some? It's the one you ordered in Singapore, your favourite?"

"You remembered?"

He sat, his expression relaxing a tad, though the wariness never left his eyes. He had no idea what he was doing here and it was time she enlightened him.

"Uh-huh," she said, barely refraining from adding 'how could I forget anything about that evening?'

He poured himself a glass of wine, his steady stare never leaving her for an instant. "This dinner invitation came as a pleasant surprise."

She almost choked on her mineral water. Not half as much of a surprise as he thought.

Replacing her glass on the table for fear of sloshing the lot, she clasped her hands to stop from fiddling and looked him straight in the eye. "I wanted us to have some quiet time together away from the office."

"Really?"

She couldn't fathom his expression. Confusion? Interest? Fear?

Nodding, she said, "I have something to tell you and it's important."

Curiosity replaced confusion in his coal-dark eyes and he leaned forward, all his attention focussed on her. "Go ahead, shoot. Though if you're gunning for a raise, forget it."

Her nervous laugh sounded hollow. "I'm pregnant and you're the father," she blurted, horrified at the inane way the words flew out of her mouth, grateful he finally knew the truth.

The smile died on his lips as he stared at her, blanching, his pallor matching the sickly beige of the walls.

"What?"

"I thought the chocolate gorging might've been a dead giveaway?"

Her false bravado petered out quickly as he didn't move a muscle, stunned into immovability, staring at her in wide-eyed shock.

"But we used protection."

"Condoms are only ninety-seven percent effective," she said, watching him compute the figures but the information not really sinking in. "I know this must be pretty shocking for you. I felt the same way when I found out—"

"How long have you known?"

She looked away, pretending to study the elaborate table setting. "Since that day I fainted."

"And you waited until *now* to tell me?"

She wouldn't have been surprised if he'd exploded or lost his temper or leaped from his seat. Instead, his cold, icy control terrified her more than any of the reactions she'd anticipated.

Reaching a hand across the table to comfort him, she flinched as he leaned away from her and out of reach.

"I wasn't sure if I wanted to tell you or not. It was a big decision to make so I wanted to take my time, think about it, and make sure I made the right one."

If he'd been pale before, he turned positively ghostly now. "And have you? Made the right decision, I mean. After all, it must've been real tough working out if you think I'm the kind of guy who can handle being told he's about to become a father or not."

He pushed away from the table so fast his chair slammed onto the floor, fury etched into every tense line of his body.

She shook her head, hating this. She should've led up to the news, broken it to him gently, tried to formulate some answers to the inevitable questions he would have. Instead, she'd spilled the news quicker than she'd dropped her guard around him that night in Singapore.

Hating the surge of tears at the mess she'd made of everything, she said, "Look, Nate, it wasn't like that. It took me a while to absorb the news, I just wanted to make sure I was doing the right thing in telling you."

Clenching his fists, he turned to face her, his frigid glare freezing her heart. "You should've told me earlier."

"Maybe," she said, sipping at her mineral water in an effort to buy some time, to give him an opportunity to calm down.

Not that she could blame him for reacting like this. She'd bawled when she first heard she was pregnant, he ranted. Everyone handled life changing news in their own way and boy, was his life in for a major change if he wanted to be a part of their child's life.

"But I can't turn back time or change the way I've gone about this, Nate. Believe me, I've thought long and hard about this and once I made the decision I really wanted you to know."

He grunted and fixed her with another icy glare before shaking his head, righting his chair, and sitting back down.

"The baby's doing fine, by the way," she said, hoping to focus his attention on the real issue here—their child—and away from how much he'd like to throttle her.

His hand shook as he reached for his wine and he took a healthy swig before replacing the glass and dropping his hand out of sight, as if embarrassed by physical evidence of his obvious shock.

"That's good. And how are you?"

"Okay, apart from the usual stuff like morning sickness."

"How far along are you?"

"Eighteen weeks."

His gaze flickered to her belly, strategically disguised behind a loose-flowing peasant top. "You can't tell."

"I'm not that big yet," she said, grateful they'd moved onto discussing the baby and away from his shock but wishing they could fall back into their natural camaraderie rather than speaking in these stilted syllables.

"A baby," he muttered, reaching for his glass again and draining half the wine before shaking his head.

They lapsed into silence, his eyes round, dark orbs in his pale face, stark in their bleakness, her gaze darting to his to ascertain the slightest change in mood.

After thirty tension-fraught seconds that felt like a lifetime she knew she had to get the rest out before she bolted upstairs and let the waterworks flow.

"I told you because I believe you have a right to know, not because I expect anything from you. Whether you want to be involved or not is entirely up to you..." she trailed off, horrified by the pain jagging across his face, his expression crumpling.

"I don't believe this," he muttered, running a hand over

his face, rubbing his eyes as if trying to erase the memory of the last few minutes, maybe erasing the memory of the night that had landed them in this co-parenting complication together.

In the face of his reaction she wanted to jump up and down and throw a tantrum to end all tantrums. She'd worked so hard to stay calm, to tell him in the right way, to understand the rollercoaster of emotion he'd stepped onto, but as he raised stricken eyes to her, she wanted to shout, wave her arms, and do anything to snap him out of it.

Struggling to keep her voice steady, she said, "What part don't you believe? The part about being a father, being involved, or the role you played in all of this?"

Some of her angst must've been audible because he sat back and folded his arms, pinning her with a stare that could turn her to stone.

"Don't patronise me," he snapped, his lips compressed in a thin, rigid line. "I'm well aware of my *role* in all of this. As for being involved, what do you want me to say?"

The fragile hold on her temper broke. "Tell me what you're thinking. Tell me how you're feeling. Tell me what I can do to make this easier. Tell me whatever you damn well please but for goodness sake stop blaming me for something that wasn't my fault!"

She thought he'd really lose it then but her tirade had an unexpected effect as his shoulders softened and he reached across the table as if to take her hand before thinking better of it.

"This isn't your fault."

"Damn right it's not," she muttered, downing the rest of her mineral water and topping up, anything to keep her hands busy and away from strangling him or touching him, whichever was worse.

"I can't tell you what you want to hear because I have no

idea what I'm feeling, let alone what I'm going to do about any of this."

She heard the sincerity in his voice but it didn't make this any easier. The man she'd hoped would stand up and be counted the moment he found out about his unborn baby wasn't feeding her the reassuring lines she'd hoped to hear.

She pushed away from the table. "I know this is a big deal and I'm well aware you need some time to absorb what I've told you. Why don't we skip dinner?"

Gratitude flickered in his eyes, the first sign of any emotion other than shock or pain. "You sure?"

Hating the way her heart sank at his first instinct to bolt, she nodded. "Go ahead. If you want to talk some more you know where to find me."

With as much dignity as she could muster, Kris headed for the stairs. She needed to get away to process her disappointment, to rationalise the disillusionment that despite the faintest hope Nate would be as thrilled as she was about this baby, he wasn't.

It didn't surprise her, yet she couldn't help the wave of sadness washing over her as she realised what a delusional fool she'd been for hoping her wretched crush could morph into something more, something they could build on and strengthen in time for the baby's arrival.

Blinking away the tears burning her eyes, she walked up the stairs, hating the finality of the front door slamming as Nate left.

Nate staggered from Kris's house like he'd drunk more than half a glass of wine, the alcohol he'd consumed sloshing around his stomach until he thought he'd puke.

Kris was pregnant.

He was the father.

He glanced back at the house, his heart clenching at the sight of the woman carrying his child silhouetted against an upstairs window before she quickly closed the blinds.

He'd known something had been different about her lately. She'd been too withdrawn, too accepting of his proposals the last few weeks, agreeing to practically everything he put forward without so much as a minor challenge. He'd attributed it to their new-found truce and in a way he'd been too happy to question it. Building a strong working relationship with her had been rewarding, fostering a friendship even more so.

He loved how they were on the same wave length. He'd have an idea, she'd put the finishing touches on it. He'd propose an amendment, she'd sanction it. They were a great team and he could envisage RX catapulting into the upper echelons of Australian broadcasting fast.

But it was more than that. He loved her quick smile, the triumph in her deep blue eyes when they made an idea happen, her loud laugh when their latest comedy series hit the top of the ratings. He loved her fierce independence and now all that was about to change, courtesy of him.

She was carrying *his* child.

Hell.

Bracing against the front fence, he took a deep breath, the crisp Melbourne air filling his lungs and hopefully clearing his head.

He couldn't do this.

No matter how much he liked Kris, he couldn't be the man she needed him to be.

Taking a chance on fatherhood equalled a risk he wasn't willing to take.

Releasing the fence, he turned away from her house and

strode down the street towards his car, his long, angry steps eating up the pavement.

If hearing Kris's news had shocked him, it had nothing on the bolt of disappointment when he realised he couldn't be the father she wanted for her child.

Yet for one, brief, crazy moment when she'd first told him he'd had a startling vision of the two of them together, his arm around her while she cradled their baby. The absurd surge of hope that their one incredible night together could've resulted in a baby had thrilled him before he'd bolted, running from his demons.

He couldn't be a father.

Reaching his car, he slammed a hand against the bonnet before getting in, hating the painful memories slashing through the fog of confusion caused by Kris's revelation.

Could he take a risk again?

No, he couldn't do it. The pain would be too great.

With his head pounding with unanswered questions, Nate gunned the engine and drove away.

He needed time to think, time to get his head around the fact he'd fathered a child and what on earth he was going to do about it.

Fifteen

Kristen took a steadying breath and stepped into Nate's office. "You wanted to see me?"

Nate nodded and beckoned her in, scribbling furiously on a notepad while he mumbled a string of 'uh-huhs' into the phone squeezed between his ear and shoulder.

She strode across his office towards his desk, wishing she had the guts to quit. It had crossed her mind several times since he'd left her place two nights ago. It would be difficult to work with him, seeing him on a daily basis, trying to pretend everything was okay, when she wanted to clobber him over the head for being a cold, callous cretin. And she'd thought her string of lousy foster mothers had been bad. At least they'd feigned interest in her at the start, whereas Nate pretended his son or daughter didn't exist.

He hadn't tried to contact her, and hadn't phoned or visited when she'd called in sick to work yesterday. His silence spoke volumes. Some people were cut out to be parents, some weren't, and until a few months ago she'd fallen into the latter category.

But that was before she'd woken up and smelt the ginger

tea; a godsend for her nausea. In a way, she should be grateful he'd shown his true colours now and hadn't strung her child along, promising birthday visits and ponies only to renege on every vow at the last minute.

She'd hated the false promises more than the lack of affection from her numerous foster parents and she'd be damned if she sat back and let her child go through the same heartache.

Cupping his hand over the mouthpiece, he murmured, "Sorry, this will only take a minute."

She nodded, not caring if he took an eternity on the phone and never spoke to her again. Sitting across from him like nothing had happened grated. She couldn't quit no matter how much she wanted to. She'd made a vow to be the best mom she could and for her that meant staying at home for the baby's first year at least, so she needed to scrounge and save every cent she could now. Besides, who would employ a pregnant woman for the next few months only?

She had no choice. She had to be the model employee, while eyeing off the steel letter opener within reach and imagining creative ways she could make her heartless boss squirm.

Nat disconnected his call, threw down his pen, and said, "Sorry about that. Interstate conference call took longer than expected."

She ignored his apology, eager to get straight to the point. The less they saw of each other, business arena or not, the better.

"What did you want to see me about?"

"This." He handed her a gilt-edged embossed invitation.

She opened it and scanned the words with little interest. "An invitation to an awards night. So?"

"We're going."

The stiff cardboard crumpled in her clenched fist like tissue paper and she forced herself to relax. "You might be. I'm not."

It took every ounce of willpower to place the balled invitation on the desk and not throw it in his face. Now, if she could manage to hold onto her temper for the few steps between the desk and the door, she'd be doing well indeed.

"Actually, we both have to go. Una and Alan are both interstate this weekend chasing up new locations for Travelogue so that leaves us to represent the station."

"Take someone else," she said, shifting her weight from foot to foot, enjoying standing over him but hating the way the straps on her stilettos cut into her ankles.

Maybe it was time to forego fashion for comfort now that she was retaining a bit of fluid? The joys of motherhood…and this was only the start.

He shook his head, reaching for the invitation and smoothing it out. "No can do. We're the head honchos of RX at the moment, we have to attend. It wouldn't look good if we didn't go, not to mention giving the rumour mill fodder for the next few months. You know we're launching an all-out attack on the ratings soon. For the sake of good PR we have to be there, no excuses."

Kristen mustered an intimidating glare, knowing she had no choice but to go along to television's biggest awards night —with him.

Damn him for being right.

Damn him for putting her in this predicament.

Most of all, damn him for eliciting the faintest thrill of pleasure at the thought of accompanying him, especially when she was supposed to be hating him right now.

"Fine. Email me the details and I'll meet you there." She turned on her heel and headed for the door without a backward glance.

"Kris?"

She bit her tongue to keep from responding and kept moving. Only a few more steps and…

"We need to talk about the baby."

She stopped dead, swivelling so fast her head spun. "Now?"

"I didn't want to have this conversation here," he muttered, running a hand over his eyes as if to obliterate a host of memories. She knew the feeling. "Poor form on my part but I can't wait until later. I don't know about you but I can't function with the two of us like this."

"We're professionals, Nate," she said, wondering if he remembered using similar words her first day when he'd belittled what they'd shared in Singapore, negating it to nothing with his nonchalance. "We need to function as best we can regardless of our personal situations."

"I deserved that, but can we talk?" He crossed the space between them in a flash, gripping her upper arms so she couldn't move, and damned if her pulse didn't leap.

Stupid pregnancy hormones.

Trying to ignore the warmth seeping into her body from his touch, she said, "Do you really want to talk about the baby here? Now? That's what the other night was about. If you hadn't run scared, that is."

His dark eyes widened and all colour drained from his face as his grip on her arms tightened. "You don't know anything about me."

Yanking free of his grasp, she sent him a scathing look. "Too right I don't. Funny thing is, I thought I did. I thought you'd be the type of guy to take some time to absorb the shock, then have the guts to at least talk to me or confront me rather than give me the cold shoulder."

"You're right, I'm sorry..." he trailed off, pinching the bridge of his nose as if he had a thumper of a headache, closing his eyes for a second before they snapped open and fixed her with a stare that could freeze nitrogen. "My reaction has nothing to do with you."

Raising an eyebrow, she tried to match his cold stare and failed. She couldn't do it when she glimpsed the devastation behind the forced coolness in his eyes and wondered what or who had put it there.

"You're wrong. It has everything to do with me. We're in this together." She reached out and snagged his hand, giving it a quick squeeze before releasing it. Touching him, even something as innocuous as a comforting hand squeeze, felt way too good. "If you want to be, that is."

Shaking his head, he perched his butt on the back of a chair, his steady stare never leaving her face. "Honestly? I don't know what I want right now."

"Oh."

"I know this is hard for you but I need some more time," he said, his grave expression imploring her to understand something she had no idea about as she wondered how her life had got so complicated.

A few months ago, the hardest decision she'd had to make was whether to wear her favourite red or black power suit to work and now, thanks to one amazing night, they'd woven an intricate web of parenthood that had them both confused and scared.

"Time. Right." She nodded, hating how squeaky her voice sounded, hating the threat of tears prickling the back of her eyelids more.

"Hey, it's okay," he said, enveloping her in a hug before she knew what was happening, and though her first instinct was to pull away she ignored it, relaxing into his embrace, wondering when she'd last been held like this.

Probably that night in Singapore when the same man had wrapped his arms around her, though back then there had been nothing but passion and heat and an overwhelming attraction. Her skin tingled at the scorching recollection and she placed her hands on his chest and eased away reluctantly.

She needed to get our of her here before she blubbered and being held by Nate, enveloped by his purely masculine scent, cradled in his strong arms, did nothing but short-circuit her brain and make her forget every logical reason she had for pushing him away.

"It's okay to be scared, you know," she said, knowing most guys would be blown away by news of impending fatherhood, yet unable to shake the feeling there was more behind Nate's reaction than fear.

He wavered between anger and coldness, fear and warmth, vacillating all over the place when he was usually commanding and in control.

"Scared? I'm terrified," he said, the serious expression on his face telling her far more than his honest words did.

There *was* something more at play here but she couldn't push him. If he hadn't made a decision about being involved with the baby yet, what right did she have to push him for answers to questions she could barely formulate?

"Hey, I'm scared too. I know it's a big deal, and I've had longer to absorb it than you have."

Cupping her cheek, he brushed his thumb along her skin, sending shivers skittering through her body. "Thanks for being so understanding."

"That's me." She stilled under his touch, her breath catching as his thumb rasped across her cheek for a brief moment before dropping away. "I don't even know if you like babies?"

Some guys did, some would run a mile at the barest hint of a goo-goo or ga-ga, and she wondered where Nate stood ever since she'd discovered the pregnancy.

He sighed and looked away, and her heart plummeted. From the moment Nate had said he wanted to talk about the baby she'd built an elaborate fantasy in her head, one where Nate loved the baby and grew to feel half of what she felt for him, wrapping them all up in one, neat, family package.

However, with his crestfallen expression and guilty gaze, he'd ripped the bow off in a swift painful action, exposing her fantasy for what it was: an empty dream without all the trimmings.

"It's complicated," he said, finally raising his eyes to meet hers again.

"Right now, complication is my middle name," she said, forcing a brittle, hollow laugh that echoed around the office.

"I want to explain it to you but I can't get into it right now. This isn't the time or place."

"Maybe later?"

Her voice sounded soft, small, shy, like a coy pre-teen asking a boy out on a date and she felt just as uncertain and gauche, hanging on his answer with hope in her heart.

"I can't. I'm flying interstate in a few hours to meet with Alan and go over the presentation stuff at the locations he selected. I'll be there all week, getting back late Sunday afternoon before the award ceremony."

Could this get any more convoluted? Maybe she and Nate weren't meant to sort things out? Maybe she'd be better off pinning her hopes on winning the lottery? A million to one chance, about the same odds she had of ever getting on the same page with Nate.

"Hey, I promise we'll talk after the awards, okay?" He tipped her chin up, his gaze warm and steady, imploring her to trust him.

Like she knew anything about trust. She'd had her scant personal belongings stolen by the biological kids at the first foster home she'd been dumped in, she'd been let down at parent-teacher interviews by her second foster mum on no less than three occasions, and the third, fourth and fifth foster homes she'd lived in had been rife with verbal and psychological abuse.

What she knew about trust equalled what she knew about babies—next to nothing.

"I don't expect anything of you," she said, stepping away, glad to re-establish some control over her personal space, hating the bereft feeling when his arms fell to his sides. "You know that's not what the other night was about. I just thought you had a right to know."

"Thanks. It means a lot."

However, he didn't look grateful. In fact, he looked downright uncomfortable, as if being a dad was the last thing he wanted.

Well, she'd make it easy for him.

"No one needs to know about this," she said, fiddling with the hem of her jacket. "I won't name you as the father on the birth certificate."

She thought she was doing him a favour. By the angry crimson flush creeping up his neck and his thin, compressed lips, she'd thought wrong.

"I'm not ashamed of this child or being recognised as the father. I just need some time."

Time for what? Time to invent excuses why he couldn't be around? Time to make himself scarce? She could've asked him but she wouldn't give him the satisfaction of knowing how much his answers meant to her.

For some strange reason, it mattered why he needed time. After the other night she'd resigned herself to being her baby's sole parent yet now, having Nate take responsibility seemed paramount. She wanted to know what was driving him, what was behind the fleeting guilt she glimpsed at times. Because maybe, just maybe, if she understood more about what motivated him, she'd have a chance of making him see how great being a parent to their child could be.

With her thoughts swinging as wildly as her emotions courtesy of her hormones, she knew she better leave before she did something crazy; like flinging herself back into his comforting arms.

"More time? Sure. We're not going anywhere." She patted her tummy, a never-ending sense of awe flooding her body at the bump already there, while his panicked glance flicked between her belly and her face.

Sheesh. How could a capable, take-charge CEO look like he was about to faint at the thought of being a father? Maybe he wasn't half the man she thought he was? And maybe she needed to give the guy a break. He said he would explain on Sunday and she had to give him the benefit of the doubt. She had no other option.

"I'll pick you up at seven?"

"Fine," she said, wondering how she'd get through the rest of the week knowing they would be discussing their baby's future after some silly award night. "See you then."

She spun on her heel and opened the door, needing some distance between her and the man who made her dream and want and crave things she had no right believing in.

"Kris?"

"Yeah?" She glanced over her shoulder, unable to fathom the intense expression casting shadows over his handsome face.

"Thanks for giving me a chance."

She flashed him a wan smile and headed out of his office, wondering if he meant a chance at being a father, a chance at explaining, or something else entirely.

Sixteen

The brass knocker clanged against Kristen's front door and she slipped on her shoes, grabbed her evening purse, and made a mad dash for the stairs, forcing herself to slow when she reached the top.

"Sorry about the bumpy ride," she murmured, caressing her belly as she descended the stairs, filled with uncertainty and fear and longing, the latter a terrible, desperate yearning for a man she knew could never be hers.

If Nate didn't want her before she was pregnant, there was no way she'd fall for any sudden change of heart. She wouldn't put it past an upstanding guy like him to want to do the right thing and include her in his grand plans for giving his child the perfect life—if he wanted involvement with his child, that is.

Pity he hadn't realised they could've had the perfect life before the baby obligated him to her.

She opened the door with a welcoming smile. "Hi, you're back."

Not the most scintillating greeting but not bad considering her mind had shut down the second she caught sight of Nate in a designer tux, his dark eyes sparkling, a sexy smile playing about his mouth, and his hands filled with a giant box covered in adorable teddy bears.

"You look beautiful," he said, the banked heat in his top-to-toe glance setting her body alight, his admiration thrilling her, as she'd spent an inordinate amount of time with her make-up, hair, and adjusting the exquisite A-line empire style dress of mauve chiffon gathered over her nicely expanding bust and falling in loose folds to her ankles.

She wanted Nate to see her as an attractive woman. She wanted him to see her as more than the mother of his child. Crazy? Definitely, though she couldn't help but wish her baby would have more than she ever had; a father to protect her, to give her advice, to beat off randy teenagers who treated her like trash because she had no parents and no one who particularly cared.

Not that she was completely delusional. She didn't expect them to be a couple but she wanted to establish a bond, a close friendship that would envelop her baby in love and security, two things she'd would've given anything for growing up.

"And this is for you."

"Thanks, come in." She stepped aside, inhaling as he brushed past her, the heady scent of his signature citrus aftershave sending her receptors into meltdown. She'd never forget that tangy freshness, a lingering reminder of the incredible night they'd shared and the way his skin had pressed against hers in so many delightful ways, branding her with his exotic scent.

"Aren't you going to open it?" He laid the box on the dining table and she nodded, overcome with momentary shyness considering the way he devoured her with his eyes, the glint of desire a potent reminder of what they'd shared, what they could share again if he threw caution to the wind and she lost her mind.

Must be the hormones again; a chapter in one of her pregnancy books clearly stated expectant mothers often found their libidos out of control. Had to be true considering all she could think about right this minute was ripping that stuffy bow tie off Nate's neck, tearing open his snowy white shirt, and burying her face against his amazing rock-hard chest.

"Kris?"

Heat flushed her cheeks and she opened the box, her heart expanding with emotion as she lifted out a giant purple stuffed hippo.

"He's gorgeous," she said, blinking back sudden tears at Nate's generosity, hoping this was the sign she'd hoped for, the sign he wanted to be a part of their child's life, and if so, knowing this would be the first of many presents for their lucky child.

"There's something in there for you too," he said, taking the hippo out of her hands when she didn't move and brushing away the lone tear that trickled down her cheek. "Though if you cry, I might have to take it back to the store."

She chuckled, dabbing under her eyes to prevent further spillage, and delved into the box, her hands searching amongst a sea of tissue paper until she encountered a small, square box.

It felt suspiciously like jewellery and she hesitated, increasingly nervous. What could this mean? Surely Nate hadn't taken his obligation to extremes and bought her a ring? He wouldn't be crazy enough to propose?

"You're one of those infuriating go-slow people on Christmas Day, aren't you? The kind who never rip off the wrapping paper all in one go to get to the good stuff?"

She flashed him a haughty stare. "Good things are worth waiting for."

"Damn right," he said, with another trademark sexy smile, notching up the temperature in the room by ten degrees at least.

With shaking fingers she flipped open the box, breathing a

sigh of relief and wonder as she poked at the tiny gold booty nestled in white satin.

"It's gorgeous," she said, marvelling at the intricate work, the perfection of it.

He cleared his throat and she wondered if he felt half as choked up as she did as the enormity of what they were doing hit home.

They were going to be parents.

There would be many opportunities like this for giving and sharing gifts with their child: birthdays, Christmas's, graduations, and beyond. Special moments to be captured like a photograph and pressed into her heart, never to be forgotten, made extra special by sharing it with a man like Nate.

"I thought you might clobber me with your laptop if I gave you jewellery so this way, you can choose to keep the charm for the baby's bracelet if it's a girl or add it to one of your own."

His tone, husky with emotion, had her avoiding his gaze. If she looked up and saw those dark eyes studying her, she'd burst into tears without a doubt.

"And if it's a boy?"

He chuckled. "Okay, you got me. I really want you to have the charm. Maybe one day you'll let me buy you the bracelet to go with it?"

"Don't push your luck," she said, with a mock pout that withered under the intensity of his stare.

"How about a charm for every milestone of the baby's?"

"Yeah, that sounds good. I can see it now. A pacifier for the first month, a teething ring for the sixth, and a potty around two?"

Actually, she liked the idea. It was sweet and thoughtful and totally Nate. "Though I draw the line at miniature gold forceps to commemorate the birth, okay?"

He laughed and slipped an arm around her waist. "Come on. We have some serious schmoozing to do."

"And later?"

His hand felt way too good resting on her hip, its warmth branding her skin through the thin chiffon, sending a powerful wake-up call to those crazy hormones that had dozed off for the last few minutes.

"I promise we'll talk," he said, dropping an all too brief, too-chaste kiss on her cheek before guiding her out the door.

Resigning herself to an interminable evening of back-slapping and fake smiles, she focussed on what really mattered about this night: Nate by her side, their baby nestled safe within her belly, and the conversation later with the potential to make or break her future.

Seventeen

"Are you having a good time?"

Kristen nodded and tried for the umpteenth time not to get lost in the dark depths of Nate's eyes.

"Actually, I am. Usually these functions are dull but with lemon meringue pie for dessert, it's taken the evening into the next realm."

Nate chuckled and pushed his dessert plate across to her. "And here I was, thinking I was the reason you were having such a good time."

"Now why would you think that?" She batted her eyelashes at him, loving every minute of this unexpected night as he laughed and pointed to the plate.

"Eat up. It's good for you," he said, dropping his voice low as he sent a pointed stare at her belly.

"If you insist," she said, needing little encouragement to devour a second serve of her favourite dessert.

However, she almost choked on the first mouthful as Nate's gaze stayed riveted to her lips, his expression hungry, though she had a sneaking suspicion it wasn't for food.

"Do you want some?"

His gaze stayed focussed on her lips a tad longer before slowly drifting upwards. "No thanks. Besides, it's much more fun watching you enjoy it."

She took her time with the next mouthful, savouring the sweet tart exploding on her tongue, her pulse racing at the avaricious gleam in Nate's eyes. Looked like her boss wanted to have his cake and eat it too.

"So what's your favourite dessert?" She needed to say something, do something, to break the sexual tension enveloping them in a cosy cocoon before she did something crazy like offer him a taste of the pie...from her lips.

"Tiramisu."

"Not bad. But not as good as this."

"I'm starting to believe it," he said, reaching across to dab at a meringue crumb clinging to the corner of her mouth.

"Thanks," she murmured, expecting him to deposit the crumb in his napkin, shocked when he lifted his finger to his mouth and ate it.

"You're right. Delicious," he said, his hypnotic stare never leaving hers as his lips curved into a knowing smile.

Kristen didn't know how long they sat there staring at each other like a couple of lovestruck teenagers, but if it hadn't been for the band starting up, she knew without a doubt she would've leaned in and kissed him.

It had been that kind of night. A night for flirting, for chatting, and for learning new things like favourite desserts. A night for growing closer, for fighting a losing battle with the escalating attraction sizzling between them. A night for doing crazy things like throwing herself at her boss.

"Would you like to dance?"

She shouldn't. If sitting next to him was sending her body into meltdown, what hope would she have wrapped in his arms?

"I'd love to," she said, happily ignoring her logic and placing her hand in his.

They strolled hand in hand to the dance-floor, Kristen grateful for his strong grip. The way her knees trembled, she wouldn't have made it two feet without his support.

"It's been ages since I've done this," Nate said, taking her into his arms and cradling her close, while she struggled not to kiss the pulse point in his throat beating at her eye level. It was so tempting...the rhythmic throb a beacon to her overstimulated imagination. It would be so easy...

"Let me guess. Favourite song?"

She tore her gaze away from his throat and tried to focus on what he was saying.

"This song? You were humming it under your breath."

Kristen had been oblivious to the music. They could've been dancing a polka and she wouldn't have known, wouldn't have cared as long as she was wrapped in this incredible man's arms.

"It is a favourite. Who doesn't like a sexy ballad to get swept away by?"

"Is that an offer?"

She held her breath, wondering how far she could tease him, wondering if she could handle the fallout. And there would be, she had no illusions about that. They hadn't discussed the baby yet. In fact, this evening was a mere prelude to the main event and she shouldn't get caught up in the romance of it.

So Nate was flirting a little? It probably didn't mean anything and she'd be better off remembering it.

"It's a ballad," she said, reluctantly disengaging from his arms as the song came to an end, and heading back to the table.

"And here I was, focussing on the sexy part," he said, falling into step beside her, the laughter in his voice audible.

She rolled her eyes as he pulled her chair out and she sat, feeling every inch a princess yet aware her prince charming could well turn into a frog by the end of the evening.

"I've had a good time tonight." Nate captured her hand, the tender expression in his eyes bringing a lump to her throat and in total contrast with the suave, confident guy who'd been teasing her all evening.

"Me too," she said, trying not to get too caught up in the moment but fighting a losing battle when he interlaced his fingers with hers.

"Want to get out of here and go have that chat?"

"You bet."

However, as they left the ballroom with their hands intertwined, Kristen wondered if she would've been better off living the fantasy a little longer.

Reality had a funny way of letting her down.

"Where are we?"

Nate turned into his street, pulled into the first house on the right and killed the engine, turning to face Kris.

"There are advantages to you not being a Melbourne girl. I can take you anywhere and it's like an adventure every time," he said, smiling as her eyes widened with curiosity, their dazzling blue a muted midnight in the dim car.

"Right now, this intrepid adventurer needs to use the bathroom desperately so unless this is your house or the house of a very good friend who'll let in a crazy woman bashing at their door, I suggest you get me to a convenience store pronto."

He smiled, enjoying her sense of humour. It was one of the things he remembered from their brief liaison in Singapore, her dry sense of humour and the ability to laugh at herself.

"Rather than have you terrorise the good folk of Middle Park on a Sunday night, I'll let you use the bathroom. Come on."

She almost ran to the front door and he unlocked it, disarmed the alarm and pushed it open, barely having time to say, "Down the hall, last door on the left," as she pushed past him and dashed down the hallway much faster than a pregnant woman should, her heels clattering along the boards.

Wondering what she'd think of his place and hoping she'd go for his plan, he flicked on the lights, illuminating the lounge room, his favourite room in the house. With its soaring ceilings, elaborate cornices and marble fireplace, it captured the period feel of the house perfectly and he often spent his limited down time in here, working from his laptop in front of the fire or reading a book while stretched out on the Chippendale sofa.

Julia had loved this room too. They'd walked into the house and known this place was perfect, making an offer to the surprised realtor on the spot.

Battling the wave of sadness that swamped him whenever he thought of her, he picked up a photo—his favourite—of them in the Whitsundays: smiling, joyous, without a care in the world. Life had been simple back then: work, play, live for the moment. Buying this house had been a big step towards their future and now, maybe it was time to start thinking about a future of a different kind.

"Who's that?"

Kris had slipped off her shoes and come up behind him, her eyes fastened on the picture frame.

"My wife," he said, replacing the photo on the granite mantel and quashing his old memories, knowing it was time to explain and eager to get to the point of this evening.

However, before he could say another word, Kris paled and slumped onto the sofa, her mouth a surprised O before her eyes clouded in confusion and flicked between the photo and his face.

"Your *wife*?" She shook her head, bewilderment and condemnation etched across her beautiful face. "It's time we had that chat, don't you think?"

Eighteen

Kristen struggled to process Nate's revelation, knowing there had to be a perfectly logical explanation.

Nate couldn't be married. She'd worked with him for months and he spent all his time at the office. Besides, he didn't seem like the kind of guy who cheated, having one night stands in foreign countries, getting women pregnant...or was he?

She knew next to nothing about him and seeing his house for the first time accentuated the fact. Though she hadn't been in Melbourne long she knew Middle Park was an upper class suburb and period homes like this cost a small fortune.

Throw in the fact the house seemed like a family home with its sprawling front lawn complete with rope and tyre hanging from an old oak tree just waiting for some child to swing from it and the sheer size of the rooms she'd seen to date, and she knew Nate had some explaining to do.

"Julia died three years ago," he said, sitting next to her on the sofa and reaching for her hand before thinking better of it.

"I'm sorry," she said softly, ashamed for jumping to

conclusions a moment ago but still annoyed she knew nothing about him.

Admittedly, it wasn't his fault. They'd agreed to forget their one night of passion, to move onto professional footing once she started working at RX, but the game plan had changed thanks to the life inside her and they'd grown closer at work despite all intentions otherwise.

"We were the cliché high school sweethearts," he said, studying his hands clasped in his lap as if they held answers to the world's problems. "We dated for an eternity, taking a break once to see other people, before realising we were meant to be together."

She remained silent, biting on her inner lip to stop crying from the pain lancing her heart. She'd wanted to know more about Nate but this wasn't what she had in mind, listening to him wax lyrical about the love of his life.

"We got married eight years ago. That picture with Jules was taken on our honeymoon."

Kris's folded arms tightened as she gave herself a comforting hug, trying to ignore the tender expression on Nate's face at his cherished memories, hating herself for being insanely jealous of a dead woman.

Right then, it hit her. She could never compete with a ghost and as much as she'd tried to deny having Nate in her life wasn't an issue, she'd been lying to herself since the moment she walked into his office and discovered the guy she couldn't forget had materialised in her life like an omen.

"You must miss her very much," she said, needing to fill the growing silence, desperate to say something before she let out an anguished groan.

He nodded, finally lifting his gaze to meet hers, and what she saw shrivelled any last residual hope she may have harboured of being anything more to him than his child's mother.

"I loved her like nothing else," he said, his gaze bright with adoration. "But she's gone and I have to move on."

Kristen didn't want to dwell on how much Nate obviously loved his wife but she needed to know what had happened, if only to satisfy some weird curiosity to discover everything that made this enigmatic man tick.

"How did she die?"

Nate's expression hardened, his dark eyes turning glacial. "A haemorrhage."

"How awful," she murmured, aware that sudden, unexpected brain haemorrhages were on the rise in young people, often with no preceding signs or symptoms.

Little wonder Nate wore an invisible cloak of sadness wrapped around his shoulders, and had since the first minute they'd met. Losing his wife so quickly, so tragically, must've hurt.

The guilt she'd sensed after they'd slept together, the way he flirted with her one minute then pulled back the next, his mood swings when they first started working together, it all made sense now. He loved his wife despite the years since her death, then she'd entered the picture and thrown him off-kilter. Sleeping with her must've been a big deal for him and he'd tried to put it behind him, only to have his night of guilty pleasure rubbed in his face when she walked through the doors of RX.

Trust her to fall for a guy caught up in the memory of his beloved dead wife.

"It's in the past." He spoke softly, as if reassuring himself, and she waited, knowing whatever she said next would sound inadequate. "But that's not relevant to what I want to discuss with you tonight," he said, louder this time and back in control. "Before we get into any of that, would you like something to drink?"

"No, I'm fine," she said, wishing he'd get to the point so

she could get out of here with what was left of her tattered dignity intact.

If she stayed a minute longer in this elegant room with pretty Jules smiling down on her, she'd start bawling.

"I've been thinking," he said, scooting closer to her, invading her personal space. "This place is too big for one person. It's designed for a family, so what do you say to moving in? Let me take care of you during the pregnancy and when the baby comes we can take it from there."

She sat bolt upright, her lower back twanging as it had been for a while now—more of those hormones apparently, softening her spinal ligaments.

"You're kidding, right?"

He shook his head, his expression dead serious and she wondered if the hormones were affecting her lucidity too. "It makes sense, Kris. Your place has those steep stairs and the larger you get the harder it will be to drag yourself up and down them. There's a master bedroom on the ground floor here, with a sitting room attached, which would make a perfect nursery."

"Master bedroom, huh?"

He had this all figured out. Up until that instant she'd assumed his offer stemmed from concern for the baby and doubts in her ability to care for it but now he'd drawn another picture, one involving the two of them reneging on their platonic deal and for one, ridiculous second, her traitorous body leapt at the idea.

"My room's upstairs so you'll have use of the whole ground floor if you want."

So he didn't want her. Who knew her expanding waistline, thickening ankles and the first hint of cellulite dimpling her previously toned thighs was a turn-off?

His offer didn't make sense. Why would a workaholic, successful guy at the top of his game want to take care of her?

She wasn't exactly helpless, far from it, and though she wanted to tell him where he could shove his offer, a small part of her loved him for making it.

Like the sun rising slowly over the horizon and bathing the earth with an illuminating glow, the first rays of realisation filtered through her, creating warmth and amazement and havoc.

She loved him?

How could that be possible when she'd never experienced the nebulous emotion let alone knew what it felt like?

Besides, it wasn't supposed to happen like this. They were a cliche, two ships passing in the night, colliding for one brief interlude before moving on. However, it looked like not only had their ships docked but they'd taken on an extra passenger, one who made them both consider crazy things.

He wanted her to move in, she suspected she felt more for him than the crush she'd previously harboured. Time to cast away and set sail for destinations unknown before her ship, along with her dreams, sunk like a stone.

"So what do you think?"

"I think you're nuts," she said, resisting the urge to reach out and comfort him when his face fell. "First you ask for more time to absorb the fact you're going to be a dad. Then you give me presents hinting at your intentions to be involved but don't actually spell it out, and now you jump to this? It's crazy."

"It's the best solution for everyone."

She raised an eyebrow, wondering if some of her irrational hormones had taken a flying leap and landed on him.

"Thanks for the offer but we can't live together. I've never lived with anyone and I value my independence as I'm sure you do. It would never work."

His jaw tightened. "We'd make it work. For the sake of the baby."

The pieces of the puzzle slid into place like the rumblings of earthquake plates moving together. "You don't think I'm capable of caring for this baby myself?"

"Don't be ridiculous," he said, his quick look-away glance speaking volumes. "I only want what's best for you."

"Cut the crap, Nate. We both know you want what's best for the baby. I'm just the incubator," she said, anger turning her words into sharp barbs intended to inflict hurt like he'd wounded her.

"That's not fair. I care about you." He reached for her hand, gripping it tightly when she tried to tug away, and used his other hand to tilt her chin up. "Listen to me. I know this pregnancy is the last thing either one of us expected but it happened and we're responsible. You wouldn't have told me about the baby if you didn't want me involved and, like it or not, I'm here to stay." His gaze bordered on desperate. "I'm sorry it took me a while to get my act together but I'm one hundred percent committed now. This baby means more to me than you could possibly know and I intend on doing everything in my power to make sure the both of you are cared for. Understood?"

The vehemence behind his impassioned declaration surprised her. It sounded like he meant it and a huge part of her was grateful her baby would have a father who would love and cherish and protect, something she never had after her parents died.

"You're hell-bent on this, aren't you?"

"Damn right," he said, his fingers warm against the tender skin under her jaw as his thumb brushed her bottom lip.

Sighing, she finally relaxed, taking hold of his hands—she couldn't take much more of that lip stroking—and squeezing both of them in hers.

"Okay, here's how it will be. I'm not moving in here no matter what you say but you can have full involvement in the pregnancy. Ultrasounds, obstetrician visits, ante-natal classes, the works. How's that for a compromise?"

"You drive a hard bargain," he said, his smile warming her down to her toes. "Sounds good. For now."

She ignored his addendum, too tired to ram her point home. She'd never move in with Nate no matter how hard he pushed or how many logical arguments he laid out. She wasn't a fool and raising a child in a home where two parents didn't love each other would do more damage than visitation rights and planned holidays.

With a weary smile, she said, "Okay then. Let's see some of this caring attitude, starting with you taking me home. I'm exhausted."

And if she didn't establish some much needed distance between them in the next few minutes she'd be curling up on his sofa—or worse, checking out the *upstairs* master bedroom.

Being with Nate felt too comfortable, too cosy, too right, and hot on the heels of the startling realisation she actually might love him, threatened to undermine her.

No matter how much he 'cared' for her, no matter how close the baby brought them, she could never compete with Julia. He'd virtually said she'd been the love of his life and Kristen had no intention of coming in a poor second. She'd had enough of that feeling growing up, always playing second fiddle to a foster parent's biological kids, always the new kid on the block as she moved from school to school, always the outsider.

She'd never be second-best again, she'd make sure of it, even if it meant breaking her heart in the process.

"Come on, I'll take you home," he said, gently pulling her to her feet, clasping her hands like he'd never let go.

More of that wishful thinking.

"Thanks, Nate. For everything," she said, knowing how

lucky she was to have a dependable guy as the father of her baby, a part of her wishing there could be more between them.

"You're welcome." He dropped a chaste kiss on her cheek, the type of kiss indicative of their relationship.

Or was it? No matter how platonic they tried to keep their relationship, there'd been shared moments in the office working on Travelogue, and at the awards function tonight, that implied otherwise. Nate at his charming best meant she had a hard time separating logic—he was just being nice to her at work functions—and her emotional side, replaying every touch, every intimate smile, and that spectacular dance when their bodies pressed close...

She should be ecstatic they'd ironed out some major issues where the baby was concerned.

Instead, as she followed him out the door of his beautiful home and to his car, she couldn't help but wish for more.

Nineteen

The sonographer paused and Kristen's heart skipped a beat, hoping nothing was wrong. "Would you like to know the sex of the baby?"

She sighed with relief as Nate's coal eyes widened, a wondrous smile spreading across his face. "What do you think?"

Kristen didn't know what you think. She hadn't known what to think for a while now. Since their chat after the awards function Nate had showered her with attention, doing considerate things like dropping by with groceries, accompanying her on walks around Albert Park Lake, even bringing her the chocolate milkshakes she craved at all hours.

A girl could get used to that sort of treatment and with every passing day she fell deeper for the man with a knack for lavishing some much-needed affection on her.

"I'm not sure. Would you like a surprise at the end?"

His gaze clouded but before she could interpret it, he said, "Honestly? I think we've both had all the surprises we can take. I'd like to know."

"Me too." She clasped his hand and turned to the sonographer. "Okay, let us have it."

The sonographer beamed as he wiped the ultrasound gel from her belly. "Congratulations. You have a healthy baby girl growing in there."

"A girl," Nate said, his voice barely a whisper as he clutched her hand.

"Wow." Kristen let the tears flow as she sat up, thanked the sonographer who grinned at them like a generous benefactor as he handed her a photo of the baby, before leaving the room.

"Bet she's as gorgeous as her mother," Nate said, tracing the baby's outline with a fingertip before leaning over and placing a soft, lingering kiss on her lips.

Kristen blinked but the tears flowed heavier as he gathered her in his arms, strong and protective, while she tried to figure out what that tender kiss had been about.

"I take it this means you're happy?" He drew away from her and brushed a strand of hair out of her face, his hand warm against her cheek for a brief moment.

"Very." She sniffled, gratefully grabbing a few tissues from the box he held out to her, wondering if she'd ever get over the urge to bawl at the slightest provocation. "We're having a girl..."

"Pretty amazing, huh?"

Amazing? Nothing came close to this overwhelming intensity of emotions: pride, awe and blinding love filled her until she could hardly breathe. Knowing the sex of the baby made it all the more real and she could now chat to her baby girl, labelling her a she rather than an unknown entity.

"This is all so unbelievable," she said, gripping his hand like she'd never let go, gazing down at her protruding belly with a growing sense of wonderment. "I have a little girl in there."

Nate reached out and rubbed his hand over her belly like a hopeful man with an old lamp wishing for a genie.

"My girls," he said, the sheen of unshed tears in his eyes almost undoing her completely as pride overpowered the momentary sadness she could've sworn she'd glimpsed earlier.

"This girl is certainly yours," she said, pushing up to a sitting position and patting her tummy, unwilling to contemplate what he meant by calling her his girl too. "Is it too early to start talking about names?"

He smiled and helped her off the bed. "No. How about we do it over dinner?"

Kristen hesitated. So far, all of time they'd spent together had been centred on the baby and she preferred it that way. No use fuelling her useless fantasies of Nate seeing her as anything other than the mother of his child, and having a cosy dinner for two wouldn't help her fertile imagination, especially when she'd heard his caring words 'my girls' and turned them into something more meaningful.

"I'll cook?"

He saw that as an enticement whereas the thought of spending time holed up in his perfect house waiting for the perfect family intimidated her more than the thought of eating with him.

Damn it, she knew falling for him would complicate matters but she hadn't expected to feel this out of her depth all the time. Lending weight to meaningless words, imagining more than friendship behind every touch or casual peck on the cheek, wishing he'd feel more for her.

"Sounds goods," she said, forcing a smile when her less than enthusiastic tone didn't convince him if the tiny frown between his brows was any indication. "As long as you don't feed me sprouts and broccoli. I'm taking a vitamin supplement and if I have one more green leafy vegetable this week, I'm going to barf."

"I thought the morning sickness had stopped ages ago?"

The teasing glint in his eyes had her chuckling with him as she padded over to a screen, clutching the back of the hospital gown threatening to give him an eyeful with every step, and slipped behind it to get dressed.

"Would you like me to bring anything?"

"Just my favourite girls."

His voice drifted over the top of the screen and her fingers fumbled with the last button of her blouse as she wondered if he had any idea of the impact his casual words had on her. She couldn't see his expression so couldn't ascertain whether he was serious or joking, especially as his tone gave little away.

Silently chastising herself for reading too much into his comments, she stepped out from behind the screen after sliding the last button home.

"Okay then, let's get back to work. Alan should have the first episode of Travelogue's new season ready for viewing." She headed for the door, brisk and business-like, the only mode keeping her focus diverted from Nate and the mixed signals he was sending her.

"Speaking of which, are you going to announce your pregnancy today?"

She nodded, glancing down at her flowing geometric patterned top in turquoise, black and camel. "I'm surprised nobody's guessed yet, with the loose clothes I've been wearing."

"You look sensational as always," he said, his admiring glance sweeping from her top to her fitted black pants with the elasticised waist and back again. "With a gorgeous body like yours, no one can tell you're pregnant unless they've seen your belly."

She fidgeted under his intense stare, flattered by his words, wishing her overactive imagination wouldn't conjure up the glint of desire in his eyes.

"Until now you're the only one who's had that privilege so let's spread the word before the rumour mill starts up."

He laid a hand on her arm as she opened the door. "You know I'm proud to be the father, right?"

"Uh-huh. But we've both agreed to keep the paternity a secret at work. It's nobody's business but ours and I don't want it affecting our professional credence."

"You sure?"

"Positive."

It was tough enough climbing the corporate ladder without having to fend off snide barbs from co-workers insinuating she was getting ahead because she'd slept with the boss.

If they only knew it had been a one-off, a distant, cherished memory she replayed at will, especially in the long, lonely hours of the morning when her bladder woke her for frequent trips to the loo and she couldn't get back to sleep for thinking about Nate.

"There is one thing you can bring to dinner tonight."

"What's that?"

"A hat."

She stared at his deadpan face, the corners of his mouth twitching with barely concealed amusement.

"A hat?"

"That's right. Now let's get back to work before the boss fires your cute butt."

She shot him a mock angry glare, secretly thrilled about his butt comment. As they left the clinic, she wondered if he would ever stop surprising her.

Twenty

"One hat, as requested." Kristen placed a misshapen red beanie on the dinner table, between the silver candlestick holders and the crystal glasses. "Now, are you going to tell me what on earth it's for?"

Nate smiled and pulled out her chair, gesturing for her to sit. "Well, you strike me as a woman of firm opinions so I thought the only way for us both to decide on a name would be to draw one out of a hat."

She laughed, a loud, genuine guffaw of a happy woman, something he'd heard more of lately, and he hoped she'd still feel that way after he dropped his bombshell on her tonight.

"Are you saying I'm stubborn?"

"Interpret it as you will," he said, grinning as he filled her glass with her preferred sparkling mineral water and lemon, increasingly grateful they could joke around like this.

They'd grown closer, had settled into a comfortable friendship; the type of friendship he valued, the type of friendship he could easily see developing into something more given half a chance.

She sipped her mineral water and replaced it on the table, her cheeky glance alerting him to another of her trademark quips. "There won't be a problem as long as you agree with me."

He chuckled. "Tell me you're not into the modern names of today. I'm a conservative guy and I don't think I can cope with my daughter being called after a piece of fruit."

"You sound like an old man."

"I am," he said, feeling every one of his thirty-six years. Gut-wrenching grief did that to a man, robbing him of optimism, joy and hope. But the remarkable woman sitting in front of him had changed all that. Courtesy of the little miracle she was carrying, he had hope for the future again and it felt great.

"You're right. I can see a few grey hairs among all that black," she said, pointing to the area around his temple. "Hope you haven't passed on the premature ageing gene to our daughter."

He grinned as he waggled a finger at her before heading for the kitchen. "Just for that, I'll serve your favourite sprouts and broccoli first."

He half expected her to follow him into the kitchen, but as he returned with plates piled high with a steaming stir-fry and saw her sitting on the edge of her seat and fiddling with cutlery, he had to admit it would take more than a few teasing words and a home-cooked meal to get her to relax.

She seemed on edge the last time she'd been here but he'd put that down to discovering he'd been married and the strangeness of the situation. However, it looked like she hadn't loosened up and if he didn't get her to unwind he had no chance of convincing her to see the wisdom of his plan.

Setting a plate down in front of her, he took a seat opposite.

"This smells fantastic," she said, inhaling the fragrant aroma of sautéed garlic, ginger and lemongrass, the three staples he used in any stir-fry.

It had been too long since he'd cooked, preferring to eat at the office or grab a quick bite on his way home most nights. He'd missed this, missed seeing the appreciative expression on someone's face as they took the first bite, the low "mmm" resonating as they forked more into their mouths.

Jules had loved his cooking, though with her long hours at the Playhouse, he'd often ended up eating alone over the years. However, seeing Kris's obvious enjoyment as she slurped up noodles, smacked her lips and shovelled the food into her mouth with surprising speed, more than made up for any reticence on Julia's part in the past.

A painful niggle of guilt wormed its way into his heart. He shouldn't compare the two women. They were very different and he'd already come to terms with the fact he needed to move on with his life.

Over the last few weeks he'd wondered if Kris's unexpected pregnancy hadn't been the catalyst he needed, forcing him to compartmentalise his memories and set about creating a new future. However, to do that he'd have to tell her the whole truth about Julia's death, and now Kris's pregnancy had advanced he couldn't do it.

He didn't want to scare her and the stress of hearing the truth now wouldn't be good for her or the baby. He'd have to bide his time and hope she'd understand once he told her everything. And he would, there was no doubting that.

He'd been torn for too long, guilt-ridden over letting another woman into his life who'd usurp Julia in his heart. However, after long nights of soul-searching, he knew Julia wouldn't want him to put his life on hold, to wallow in grief and self-pity. She'd always lived life to the fullest, throwing herself into their relationship with as much passion as she had for her roles on stage.

"Life is meant to be gobbled like a scrumptious chocolate cake, not nibbled around the edges," she used to say, and he could almost sense her now, silently egging him on to set aside the past and focus on the future.

"You haven't touched yours," Kris said, pointing to his plate while she dabbed at her mouth, her apologetic glance flicking between her plate and him. "Meanwhile, I've just scoffed a meal in two seconds flat."

"You know there was broccoli in that?"

Her hand flew to her mouth in mock horror. "Really? Is that what those little green tree-shaped things were?"

He laughed, pushing his noodles around the plate before giving up and resting the fork on the side. No use pretending he had an appetite. Besides, he doubted he could force a mouthful of food past the giant lump stuck in his throat.

"What's wrong?"

Realising there was no time like the present, he swapped seats, sliding into the stiff-backed chair next to her. "Nothing's wrong. But I want to talk to you about something."

"By the look in your eye, it sounds serious."

"It is." He took hold of her hand, small and soft, hoping she felt one iota of what he felt for her. It was the only way he could convince her to go through with this. "I was planning to wait until later but I can't concentrate on anything else."

Her eyes widened, depthless blue pools a man could drown in. "You're starting to scare me."

"Sorry, that's the last thing I want to do."

Taking a deep breath, he tried not to blurt out the words he'd silently rehearsed the entire afternoon.

"I know this is going to sound crazy, especially after you refused my offer to move in, but I want you to consider this carefully. It's the best thing for the baby, to surround her with both parents, especially in the early formative years. She needs to feel loved and I think we can give that to her. Together."

Gripping both her hands, staring into her incredible eyes, and hoping he was doing the right thing for them all, he said, "Kris, will you marry me?"

Twenty-One

Kristen stared at Nate in horror, certain she'd heard a proposal spilling from the lips she spent way too much time fantasising about but her brain was having a problem computing it.

"*Marry* you?" Shaking her head, she took shallow breaths, trying not to hyperventilate at a time when she needed her wits the most.

He squeezed her hand, his voice steady when she felt like screaming. "I know it's out of the blue and probably the last thing you expected, but I really want us to make a go of this. To try and be a family for our daughter."

Kristen gritted her teeth so hard her jaw ached. She couldn't believe he was doing this to her again. First the move-in-and-let's-play-happy-families scenario and now this?

Hating the quiver in her voice, she said, "Do you love me?"

The widening of his eyes and quick look-away spoke volumes. "I care about you, Kris. Surely you know that?"

Numb with pain, she said, "I know you care but a

marriage needs more than that. And you mean well, but you've presented your proposal with all the flair of a business deal and it's not enough. You want to take care of me and the baby? Fine. You want to lavish our daughter with love? Fine. But we don't have to be married or live together for you to do that."

"We have a solid foundation for a marriage. We could build on it. We could—"

"I can't marry you, Nate. I'm sorry." She stood, not surprised he released her hands, and she moved across to the fireplace, staring into the flames while she blinked away tears before turning to face him again. "I know you want what's best for the baby. I do too, but children pick up on emotions around them and I don't want our daughter realising the only thing keeping her parents together is her."

"It wouldn't be like that," he said, his tone low and imploring as he crossed the room to stand beside her. "Surely you feel something for me? Enough to take a chance on building a future for our daughter? To take a chance on seeing what develops?"

Pain ripped through her at the bleakness in his eyes.

Feel *something*?

She felt everything for him.

She picked up her denim jacket lying on the back of the sofa and shrugged into it. "I'm sorry, Nate. Feeling *something* isn't enough and I'm not prepared to sit around waiting for whatever we feel for each other to maybe or maybe not develop into more. Respect, admiration, attraction, whatever we've got right now, isn't enough. I deserve more than that. We both do. I need more and I won't settle for anything less."

Willing her legs to move towards the door, she half-expected him to stop her. Even with the empty ache spreading through her heart as every step took her further away from him, she wanted him to stop her, to tell her this was a huge mistake, that he did love her and marrying her, becoming a real family, was the most important thing in his life.

He didn't stop her and the hollow slam of the door echoed the slam of her heart as she shut away her love for the man who'd broken it without trying.

———

"What's this?" Nate looked up from the pile of documents on his desk and held up her letter the minute Kristen entered his office and slammed the door.

Damn it, she'd decided to play this cool, to be professional to the end, but seeing him sitting behind his fancy desk with a smug expression and a raised eyebrow, as if he didn't quite believe her letter was serious, spiked her temper in a second.

"Have you read it?"

"Uh-huh."

To her annoyance, he screwed it into a ball and lobbed it into the trash three metres away.

Forcing her hands to unclench, she marched over to his desk, taking small satisfaction in standing over him. "You really should keep important documentation like resignation letters for the HR department. They'll want stuff like that for employee records."

Folding his arms, he leaned back in his chair and fixed her with a benevolent smile. "I'm not accepting your resignation."

"You have no choice." Her voice rose and she calmed it with effort, the same effort it took not to lean over the desk and wipe that grin off his face. "I don't want to get into this with you."

She wished he was more rattled, hating how he didn't take her seriously. She'd thought long and hard about this since his proposal, and working with him on a daily basis with that hanging between them made her life unbearable. She couldn't stand another second, let alone another month.

"What about your maternity leave?"

Squaring her shoulders, she said, "What about it? If I leave it doesn't matter, does it? I'll be on permanent maternity leave until I find another job."

His eyes narrowed and she saw his right hand flex. At last, she'd scored a reaction. "You don't have to do this, Kris."

"Damn right I do," she said, finally taking a seat. It was hard to maintain a tough stance when her feet were killing her courtesy of swollen ankles.

"Is it so hard working with me?"

Her gaze snapped to his, surprised by the hint of vulnerability she glimpsed in the dark depths, and hating how her heart thawed at the sight of it.

"Honestly? Yeah, it is."

"I thought we'd moved past the proposal?"

"You might've," she muttered, hating the lurch of her heart as she recalled that fateful evening, the evening when for one second she'd almost believed all her dreams had come true.

However, remembering his business-like marriage proposal rankled no matter how much he cared, no matter how many different ways he showed it. Seeing him on a daily basis was emotionally exhausting and she couldn't do it anymore.

"Let's call it quits, okay?"

Nate pushed out of his chair and moved around the desk to squat next to her and grab hold of her hand. "Are you just talking about the job?"

"Uh-huh," she said, surprised by the devastation in his eyes, the sad twist to his mouth.

"Why walk away from a job you love and are great at if

you're still going to see me anyway?" Shaking his head, he grabbed her other hand until she had no option but to face him, to listen to him. "Obviously I'm the problem here, the problem you're trying to escape, but I'm not going anywhere. I'm going to be a part of the baby's life, so why run away? Why now?"

Because I love you.

Because it hurts too much seeing you every day, thinking about what we could have if you'd give us a real chance, not some marriage based on obligation.

Because I want us to be the family you spoke about, for real.

Hating the treacherous warmth seeping from his grip through her body, she pulled her hands out of his. "Because it's too hard," she finally said, barely a whisper as she stared at her folded hands lying in her lap.

"It doesn't have to be," he said, placing a finger under her chin and gently tipping it up until she had no option but to meet his eyes.

"I don't want you to go, Kris. You mean too much to me."

"Don't you mean the baby?"

He didn't deserve her bitter response, not when she could see the genuine tenderness in his eyes. To his credit, he didn't back down, even when she pushed away his finger and broke the tenuous contact binding them.

"I'm not talking about the baby. I'm talking about you and me."

Straightening, he stalked to the trash, pulled out her resignation letter, smoothed it out and laid it on the desk in front of her.

"I've tried to be as honest as I can with you about everything. And I'm not letting you leave here without a fight. So here's your letter. If it's gone by the time I come in tomorrow, I'll take it you've come to your senses. If not," he shrugged into his jacket and picked up his briefcase. "be prepared to do battle. I'm not letting my star executive producer walk out of here no matter what she thinks."

"You're...you..."

He silenced her indignant sputtering with a swift, fierce, but all too brief kiss on the lips, before sending her a smug grin and strolling out the door.

Twenty-Two

Nate entered the conference room carrying a huge basket filled with baby stuff, pasting a smile on his face as he fought his way through the crowd surrounding a radiant Kris.

"For the mom-to-be," he said, placing the basket on the table, wondering how long before he could make a run for it.

Having a baby shower before Kris left had been Hallie's idea but now that the day had arrived he couldn't be less happy if he tried.

He'd miss her.

A lot.

Feeling something just isn't enough. Her words from the night he'd proposed haunted him, taunting him with their finality, implying she might feel something for him but it was nowhere near enough to get her to marry him.

Until her refusal, he'd had no idea how badly he wanted to provide a stable home for his daughter, how much he was willing to risk in opening up to the possibility of more than a platonic relationship with Kris.

Being married would've given him the opportunity to take

things slow, to break down the carefully erected barriers around his heart, and maybe, just maybe, take a chance on more than 'caring' for a woman again.

But Kris didn't see the logic in his proposal or didn't feel enough for him to take a chance and no amount of wishing things could be different would change that.

She said she deserved more than he was willing to give and sadly she was right but he couldn't lie to her. He had no idea what would happen if he opened his heart to another woman and he'd been as honest as he could be.

For Kris, it wasn't enough.

"Thanks," she said, smiling up at him, the familiar twinkle in her eyes.

Ever since he'd called her bluff over her resignation a month ago, they'd entered a weird impasse in their relationship. He'd challenge her, she'd fire back. She'd tease him, he'd want to kiss her senseless, until he remembered he had to keep things in the office professional.

If she'd wanted to bolt after his proposal, it didn't take an Einstein to figure out what she'd do if he hauled her into his arms as he'd wanted to do on a daily basis.

"Hey, boss. How about you propose the toast?" Hallie thrust a champagne flute into his hand and he blinked, annoyed by the coy smile playing about Kris's sensual mouth as if she could read his thoughts.

Straightening, he addressed the room as he had many times over the last few months. "Since I've taken over here at RX, I've been constantly impressed by the work ethic and camaraderie shown by all of you, as demonstrated today in this great turn-out for Kristen's farewell and baby shower. As you all know, she's agreed to take a year's maternity leave and I'm hoping to lure our star executive producer back to the fold then."

Cheers greeted his announcement and he smiled at Kris, his heart pounding as she returned it.

"She's been a great asset to the RX team and I know you'll join me in wishing her and her bundle of joy all the best." He raised his glass in her direction, watching her throat move almost convulsively as she sipped at her apple cider, her expression stoic.

"Since you're so impressed with our work ethic, boss, does this mean you'll be shouting the bar at Manic Monday tonight?"

Several people cheered Hallie's cheeky question and he held up his hand to quieten them. "While our erstwhile receptionist seems to think this station has a bottomless pit of funds, I'm willing to shout each of you a drink tonight if you get back to work within the next five minutes and actually get something done in the next two hours before knock-off."

As expected, the conference room cleared within five minutes, people draining champagne and taking their cake plates with them. His staff may be the most productive, loyal lot around but they loved a drink to unwind after work on a Monday.

Once Hallie, the last straggler, had given them a cheeky smile and closed the door behind her, Nate sat next to Kris and topped up her glass with cider.

"How are you doing?"

"A little tired," she said, resting her folded arms on her belly.

Exhausted more like it, he thought, noting the dark smudges of fatigue under her eyes despite the careful use of cosmetics.

"You sure you're up for the last pre-natal class tonight?"

"Positive." She nodded, her blonde hair falling around her shoulders, longer and softer now than when she'd first started work. "They're going over the birth options and I really want to be there for that."

"Want me to pick you up?" He expected her to refuse, as she had on the previous five occasions, but to his surprise she nodded.

"That would be great. I've been feeling pretty lousy today. For a while there I thought I'd have to miss my own baby shower."

"Nothing serious?" His calm voice belied a surge of worry. Now that she'd mentioned it, she didn't only appear exhausted, she looked downright ill. Despite the sassy glance she'd sent him earlier, her eyes now seemed dull and could be indicative of something more serious, like a virus, and her pallor couldn't be disguised by blush.

She rubbed her belly and grimaced. "No, I'm okay. Just the odd Braxton-Hicks contraction."

That's when it hit him. She was scared, probably petrified, by the fake contractions that sometimes preluded the real thing.

He reached for her hand instinctively, desperate to reassure her. "It's going to be okay. Trust me."

Her gaze settled on their hands, her body inert before she finally turned her hand over in his and hung on for dear life. "I do."

Two little words, whispered into the fraught silence, encapsulating every hope and dream he'd had for the two of them. He'd wanted to hear her utter those words in a different context but for now they would have to do. He needed to be present for her, to shunt aside his fears as her due date grew near, and concentrate on being strong for both of them.

"You stay here and I'll load this stuff into your car, then drive you home, okay?"

She nodded and slowly withdrew her hand from his. "Nate?"

Resting a basket filled to the brim with soft toys on his hip, he said, "Yeah?"

"I couldn't have done this without you."

He smiled, sensing the desperation underlying her words, knowing he needed to reassure her now more than ever.

"Yeah, you could. You're a superhero. You just hide your cape and wear your underwear on the inside."

He headed for the door, thankful he'd made her smile, hoping it stayed there for the weeks ahead leading up to the birth.

Twenty-Three

Kristen tried to concentrate as the nurse facilitator droned on and on about epidurals, forceps, episiotomies, and a host of other not-so-fun things she might have to cope with at the birth of her baby.

Women in the group winced and crossed their legs for most of the talk; incredibly funny, considering it was way too late for that. As for the men, most had paled when the nurse passed around the forceps and some had left the room when the actual birth video screened.

Nate had stayed by her side through it all, his expression focussed and resolute as if he didn't want to miss a second. She could've admired him if it weren't for the constant nagging ache in the middle of her back and the fact she blamed him for putting it there.

Irrational? Maybe, considering she'd been more than a willing participant in their unforgettable night in Singapore, but as the birth grew closer and her fears escalated accordingly, it only seemed fitting to blame every little thing on the guy who had gotten her into this predicament.

"How are you holding up?" He murmured as the nurse passed around lifelike dolls to the couples, along with a bundle of nappies.

"So far so good," she said, handing him the doll with all the finesse of a rugby player making a pass. "Though I think it's your turn for nappy duty tonight."

"No worries."

With a confident grin, he whipped off the doll's threadbare clothes and folded a nappy as they'd been taught last class. However, his skilful demonstration came undone as he attempted to fasten the nappy, involving some slick manoeuvring of the doll's leg, resulting in it detaching from the body.

"Oops. I better keep a close eye on you when it's time for you to look after the real thing."

She'd meant it as a joke but Nate didn't laugh. In fact, he didn't move or do much of anything apart from stare in horror at his hand holding the leg.

"Hey, it's no big deal. These dolls are worn out. You'll be great with our daughter."

They still hadn't got around to naming the baby yet and she knew they'd have to tackle that potentially touchy subject in the coming weeks. Though she hadn't told him yet, she did favour alternative names rather than stodgy old favourites and it looked like another battle loomed on the horizon.

"I need to get out of here," he murmured, thrusting the doll's leg at her, his eyes stark and haunted. "I'll meet you outside in half an hour."

"Nate, it's okay—" She didn't get to finish her sentence as he fled the room like a man with a million demons on his tail, leaving her holding a one-legged doll and trying to ignore the ten pairs of curious eyes focussed on her.

So he'd run out on her? It wasn't like it hadn't happened to her before; she'd been consistently let down by people during her life. Though Nate had never abandoned her or let her down, unless she counted the crucial fact he didn't love her. They'd pretended his proposal never happened over the last month but as the baby grew and it was increasingly difficult to sleep, she often thought back to that night and played the 'what if' game.

What if he'd felt more for her?

What if the proposal had been fuelled by love and passion rather than caring and obligation?

What if she was the type of woman to not give a damn anyway and take what he offered?

Many couples had marriages based on a lot less than the mutual respect and caring she and Nate shared, but she couldn't do it. She couldn't tie herself to a man who didn't love her, no matter how solid and dependable he was.

Besides, she'd promised to be the best mother she could be and that meant being happy and content, two emotions she'd have to fake if forced to live in a sham marriage with the man she loved.

"Is everything all right, dear?"

Kristen nodded at the kindly nurse with concern in her eyes. "Yes. I'm fine."

The nurse looked doubtful as she moved on to the next couple, casting the occasional glance over her shoulder as if Kristen might follow suit and bolt—waddle—out the door after Nate.

Sorely tempted, she settled back in her seat, constantly wriggling as the pain in her back fluctuated from bearable to agonising, not hearing a word the nurse said as her thoughts centred on Nate and the way he'd reacted to the doll breaking.

That was no ordinary reaction. He'd freaked out to the extent he couldn't stay for the rest of the class. She might've expected that reaction at the actual birth but losing it over a doll's leg?

Uh-uh, there was something drastically wrong, and

though she couldn't fathom his reason for bolting like a dad who'd discovered he had quadruplets rather than twins, come the end of the class she'd find out.

Twenty-Four

"Do you mind telling me what your vanishing act was all about?" Kristen barged up to Nate in the hospital foyer, stopping short of jabbing his chest with her finger. "Because the way I see it, there's no way you'd get that upset and miss the rest of the class over breaking a doll, so what's going on?"

He could barely meet her eyes. "Let's talk somewhere more comfortable."

He took hold of her hand, and rather than pulling away as was her first instinct, she fell into step beside him. No use letting pride get in the way of a little support, especially considering her back chose that moment to remind her it didn't like carrying around the extra fourteen kilos.

Once they'd settled in the car, she faced him. "Don't you dare think about starting that engine until you've explained what happened back there."

"We can talk at your place," he said, running a hand over his eyes as if to block her out.

Fat chance.

"No way. Start talking."

"It's complicated." He fiddled with his keys, jiggling them in his hand until she plucked them away.

"You've tried that one on me before and as an excuse, it's sounding as tired as I feel."

Sighing, he closed his eyes for a moment and rested his head against the headrest. "When I told you Julia died, I didn't tell you everything."

Kristen's heart stilled at his audible pain.

"She was pregnant at the time."

"Oh, Nate." Kristen reached out blindly, wanting to touch him, to comfort him, to do whatever she could to take away the agony he must be going through.

Opening his eyes, he turned to face her, his expression unreadable in the darkness of the car. "I know I over-reacted back there. Stupid, how such a small, insignificant thing like that can ram home how inadequate I felt over Julia's death and the fact I couldn't save her or our child."

"You can't blame yourself for what happened. I can't begin to understand the heartache you must've gone through losing your wife and child but medical stuff happens. Stuff you can't explain or change or fix no matter how much you want to." Grasping his hand tightly, her heart aching for him, she injected as much warmth, as much love as she dared, into her voice. "And for what it's worth, I'm here for you and I know you're going to be a great dad for our daughter."

"Thanks."

She caught a glimmer of his smile in the wan light and squeezed his hand, wondering what else he had to say when he opened his mouth before quickly shutting it again.

"Is there something else?"

"I'm worried about the birth," he said, his voice unsteady as he raised worried eyes to hers. "I hate feeling out of control when I can organise the rest of my life with ease. It's tough."

Her heart turned over at his honest response. She understood exactly how he felt. Bordering on being a control freak herself, she wasn't rapt about the unexpected scenarios the nurse had mentioned in the birthing class.

"So you're admitting you're scared too?"

She thought he'd lie, do the macho thing and fob her off with some lame platitude. Instead, he surprised her by taking hold of her other hand, his grip tight.

"Terrified," he said, his expression matching how she felt perfectly.

"What happened to you being the solid one for us both? What about all those 'she'll be right' pep talks you've given me?"

He shrugged, a hint of a smile playing about his mouth. "As I remember, you told me to shut up the last time I tried to give you a confidence boost, though in much more blunt terms."

She smiled, releasing his hands before she did something stupid, like haul him over the console and hug him to death. "Must've been the hormones talking."

"We're going to get through this. You know that, right?"

She rolled her eyes, determined to lighten the mood. She had enough to worry about without Nate freaking out, especially when she'd grown to depend on him. "Of course we will. As long as you don't buy our little girl any dolls for Christmas, we'll be fine."

He finally smiled, a rueful expression erasing the lines fanning from the corner of his eyes like a worry map. "You're not going to let me forget that episode with the doll's broken leg, are you?"

"Nope."

"If you bring it up at our daughter's twenty-first, I may have to ensure you never work in the television industry again."

She waved away his remark with a smirk. "I'll be a millionaire by then, living off my name alone, consulting for the best producers in town."

"Yeah?"

"Yeah," she said, realising they hadn't traded banter like this in way too long. They'd been too busy treading on eggshells around each other, all their conversations focussed on the baby and little else. This felt good. Way too good, and the baby kicked at that precise moment as if reminding her it couldn't last.

"I like a confident woman," he said, holding out his palm for the keys.

"And I like a man who admits to a doll phobia," she said, plopping the keys into his hand and chuckling when he snatched them away, inserted them in the ignition and started the car with a roar.

"I'm never going to live this down, am I?"

"You said it," she said, settling into the plush leather seat, content to concentrate on the inner glow fuelled by the thought of them being together at their daughter's twenty-first.

A lot could happen in that time, including convincing the gorgeous man beside her what he was missing out on by not giving them a chance. A *real* chance based on love rather than an obligatory proposal reeking of old-fashioned chivalry.

Time would tell, and for now it was enough to hope and dream and look forward to a future filled with a bouncing baby girl and Nate by her side.

Twenty-Five

Nate knocked on Kris's door for the second time, pounding the brass knocker several times before peering through the sheer curtains lining the front window.

A strange sense of foreboding crept through him as he scanned the empty room, wondering why she wasn't answering the door. She'd been expecting him, had chewed him out for five minutes on the phone earlier about installing the car seat before her due date next week and he'd hurried over, the slightly hysterical edge in her voice filling him with concern.

When he rapped on the window and got no response, he vaulted the side fence and ran to the back door, relieved to find the flimsy catch unlatched.

"Kris? You in here?"

He entered the kitchen, trying to keep a lid on his skyrocketing blood pressure. There could be a perfectly logical explanation why she hadn't answered the door: she could be taking a bath to ease her back pain or making another of her frequent toilet stops.

However, as he entered the hallway and spied her inert form slumped over the bottom stair, unadulterated panic shot through him and he ran towards her, haunted by a terrifying sense of déjà vu.

"No, no, no," he muttered, feeling for a pulse in her neck, sagging with relief when he found one.

After gently turning her into the coma position, he fumbled for his phone and dialled an ambulance, praying harder than he ever had in his life.

Brushing back her hair, he bent over her, whispering in her ear. "Kris, I know you can hear me. Everything's going to be fine. We have a precious baby girl waiting for her mum to wake up and give me another verbal spray about something I've done wrong so come on. Wake up, you hear me?"

Her eyelids flickered and for a second hope overrode the adrenalin surging through his body. But she didn't open her eyes. She didn't do anything apart from lie there, too still, too lifeless.

He knew he should check for blood but he couldn't do it. Seeing her like this was tearing him apart, he couldn't face the possible evidence of losing their baby too.

He heard incoming sirens and he pressed a kiss to her lips before rushing to the door and opening it for the paramedics.

"She's in there." He pointed to the woman he loved, frozen like a statue as they went to work on her, their precise movements calming yet terrifying at the same time.

Right then, it hit him, as he watched the paramedics fiddle with pressure cuffs and stethoscopes and a host of intimidating medical paraphernalia.

He loved her.

Wholeheartedly. Unreservedly. Terrifyingly.

And as much as he loved their unborn daughter, even if the unthinkable happened and she didn't survive, he would still love Kris and everything she'd become to him.

"How many weeks is she?"

"Thirty-nine," he said, knowing the baby could be delivered safely now.

If the baby was still alive.

At that moment, Kris's eyelids fluttered open, her bright blue eyes fixing on him.

"What's going on?" she said, struggling to sit up, confusion clouding her beautiful features.

"I'm guessing you fainted?" the older paramedic said, casting Nate a look between exasperation and congratulation.

"Not again," she said, rolling her eyes and sending a horrified look at her dress hiked up around her waist. "Is the baby all right? Did I do any damage when I slumped to the floor?"

The female paramedic laid a reassuring hand on her arm. "The baby is fine. The heartbeat is steady and strong."

"Thank goodness." Kris's whisper slammed into him, reinforcing his overwhelming relief, and he crossed the short distance separating them, crouching down to her level, torn between wanting to bundle her into his arms and hug her breathless and shaking her silly for scaring him like that.

"Do you have gestational diabetes?" The female paramedic squatted next to him and took Kris's blood pressure while the other paramedic repacked the emergency case.

Kris shook her head and he forced himself not to reach out and smooth the tousled blonde waves back from her face.

"No, though my blood sugar has dipped a few times. The doc told me to pop a jelly bean or barley sugar every time I felt woozy. I was heading to the kitchen when I must've passed out."

"Well, your blood pressure's fine now, as are the rest of your vitals." The paramedic slid the pressure cuff off her arm and tucked it away in her jacket of a hundred pockets. "You should be fine, but take it easy, okay? This bub wants its mom in tip-top shape when he or she makes its grand entrance into the world."

"She," he and Kris said in unison, their eyes meeting, hers luminous, his relieved.

He'd never known relief until she'd opened her eyes a few minutes ago, backed up by the paramedics pronouncing the baby was fine. Whatever the cause of her collapse, he knew one thing for sure. He wasn't going to let her out of his sight ever again.

She could kick, she could scream, she could threaten to tell every media outlet in Australia about the infamous doll incident and his subsequent freak out, but he wasn't taking no for an answer this time.

They belonged together, now and forever.

"Right, we'll leave you folks to it," the male paramedic said, flanking Kris's other side as they helped her to her feet and to the nearest chair. "Take care."

"Thanks," she said, colour returning to her cheeks as Nate sent her a glare which read 'sit there and don't move a muscle' before escorting the paramedics out the door and returning to the lounge room.

"You look mad." She pointed to the chair next to her and he marvelled at her resilience, while smiling at her bossiness.

Nothing kept this woman down: a move from one country to another, discovering the man she probably wanted to forget was her new boss, an unexpected pregnancy, and the odd collapse thrown in for good measure. She was remarkable. Little wonder he'd fallen for her even if it was the last thing he wanted.

"I'm not mad," he said, taking a seat next to her, wondering if he should go for the direct approach—which he'd tried and failed before—or lead into it gently.

She leaned across and placed a hand on his forearm, her palm cool against the heat of his skin. "I know I must've given you a scare when you came in and found me like that. But I'm fine. The baby's fine. No use getting that look."

"What look?"

The corners of her mouth twitched and he could hardly restrain himself from closing the short distance between them and covering her lips with his. "The same look you got before you asked me to move in with you, the same look before your proposal." Her other hand reached up and she traced a slow, sensuous path between his brows. "You get this funny little frown line right here. It alerts me to the fact you're about to say something profound."

"I am."

He missed her touch as she sat back and folded her arms, resting them on her swollen belly.

"Okay, let me have it. What is it this time? You think I should have a water birth? You've hired a police escort to take us to the hospital when the time comes? You—"

"You talk too much," he said, leaning across the chair and kissing her, angling his head for better access, his libido firing on all cylinders as she melted under him, opening her mouth to him.

He could've kissed her forever, her lips warm and pliant, her hands clutching his shirt like she'd never let go. If he had his way, she wouldn't.

The fire they'd created in Singapore had been nothing like this mind-blowing, raging inferno that spread like wild-fire and threatened to consume them both.

He'd tried denying the sizzling attraction back then and his good intentions had ended up like his discarded underwear on the floor of his hotel room.

He'd never believed in fate. Yet some indefinable force had led him to Kris, to this shattering moment when his heart unfurled and swelled with love, a feeling he'd shunned for too long.

Whatever had brought this amazing woman into his life, he couldn't believe his luck and he'd make sure she knew it every day.

"Whoa." Her fingers relaxed their death-grip and her palms splayed across his chest as she pulled back slightly, her lips plump and her eyes wide with shock. "What was that about?"

"Would you believe I thought you needed mouth-to-mouth?"

She smiled. "Try again, wise guy."

"Would you believe I've just eaten a jelly bean and thought you could use the sugar boost?"

She arched an eyebrow. "Come on, you can do better than that."

"Would you believe I love you, I want to marry you, and I want us to be a real family? You, me and our daughter?"

Her face fell, her eyes hardening to icy blue as she dropped her hands into her lap. "That's not funny."

"It's not a joke," he said, desperate to make her see how genuine he was, how much she meant to him. "I want us to be together."

He'd known she'd be a hard sell but her frigid expression would freeze him solid if he were wet.

"You'd do anything to protect this baby, wouldn't you?"

"No...yes...hell." He rubbed a hand over his face, wishing this was a bad dream and he'd wake up to find Kris nestled in his bed, smiling at him with love and affection. "Yes, I'd do anything to protect our baby but this isn't about that. This is about us. This is about me falling under your spell in Singapore. This is about me being unable to sleep at night for thinking about you, for missing you, for wanting more for us but too scared to grab it and face my feelings."

Her glacial expression thawed. "I don't get it. Why didn't

you tell me any of this before? Why did you let me walk away after I knocked back your last proposal?"

He sighed, knowing it would come to this. Knowing he'd have to tell her the whole truth if he wanted to win her love. "You know that handbag resembling a suitcase you had when I first met you? Well, I carry around enough baggage to make that look like a thimble."

Sadness flickered in her eyes. "This has to do with Julia, doesn't it?"

He nodded, regret filling him that he hadn't told Kris everything. It would've saved him a lot of trouble and a lot of heartache. He'd loved Julia but what he felt for Kris went way beyond that. In a way, the depth of his feelings scared him beyond belief but now he'd come to his senses he couldn't stand for them to be apart a second longer.

Before he could speak, she placed a finger on his lips and shushed him. "You don't have to say it. I know she was the love of your life. I know you'll never get over her. You say you love me, but can you look me in the eye and say it's the same love you had for her?"

"No, it's—"

"Owww!" Her howl ripped through the air, chilling his blood as she doubled over and gripped under her belly, all colour draining from her face.

"The baby?"

She nodded, her lips turning blue from being compressed so hard before another guttural groan tore from her throat.

"Damn it, wish those paramedics had stuck around," he muttered, kneeling in front of her and capturing her face in his hands. "Kris, look at me. Is your hospital bag upstairs in your bedroom?"

"Yes," she gritted out, pain contorting her features while he attempted to smooth away the lines.

"Okay, I'll grab it and then we'll head to the hospital. I

need you to breathe through the contractions and try to relax."

"Just get the bloody bag," she said, every ounce of her pain concentrated into the killer glare she shot him.

He ran up the stairs, knowing her language might get a lot more flowery before the birth was over.

The birth...he was going to be a dad...hell.

He sprinted into her room, grabbed the small wheelie suitcase near the door, and headed down the stairs taking two at a time.

Not surprisingly she hadn't moved, gripping the arms of the chair so hard her knuckles stood out.

"How far apart are they?"

"I don't know, I'm not wearing my watch," she said, her petrified gaze locking with his, and he dropped a quick kiss on her head before bolting to his car, shoving her case in the trunk and running back to the house.

It was the damndest thing, almost as if he were having an out of body experience, watching a crazy man running all over the place, totally focussed on the woman waddling down the path, leaning heavily on his arm and doubling over as they reached the car.

"Come on, sweetheart. We'll be at the hospital in five minutes," he said, easing her into the car as another contraction hit and she almost broke his wrist with her grip.

"Make it two," she said, resting her head back and closing her eyes, one hand rubbing the top of her belly while the other circled beneath.

Nate considered himself a careful driver but when Kris let out the loudest groan yet he floored it, cutting lanes, copping one-finger salutes and tooting horns as he screeched into the hospital and pulled up in front of the ER.

"Hurry." She moaned, her head thrashing side to side, and he made a dash for the entrance, grabbing the first nurse he could find and pointing to his car. "The baby's coming. Please do something."

To the nurse's credit, she made frantic hand signals at the receptionist who summoned an orderly with a wheelchair and a doctor within two seconds.

"Calm down," the nurse said. "Everything's going to be all right."

Was it? He had no idea. This was happening so fast and he hadn't had a chance to tell Kris how much she meant to him. What if something happened to her? What if she went through this daunting experience thinking he loved her less than Julia?

"Nate!" Kris's ear-piercing scream had him sprinting after the wheelchair and into a small room off the ER.

The next five minutes happened in a blur as a grim-looking doctor bustled in, checked Kris's dilation and pronounced her four centimetres dilated. Only four? *Four*? A little piece of Nate curled up and died as he held her hand, watching her grunt and sweat and moan her way through the next contraction, knowing there would be many more before their daughter was born as the information he'd absorbed in pre-natal class came back.

"The cervix needs to be dilated ten centimetres before the next phase begins." He distinctly remembered the midwife conducting the classes teaching them that, the figure sticking in his memory because ten centimetres sounded awfully big to him.

Kris whimpered and he squeezed her hand, wishing he could do more, wishing he could take away her pain, wishing he could do something other than sit here like a useless dummy.

As if reading his mind, she fixed him with an angry stare. "You being here is enough so don't go getting any ideas to bolt on me, you hear?"

He smiled, trying not to wince as pain contorted her beautiful features. "I'm not going anywhere, even if you call me every name under the sun."

She gritted her teeth and gripped his hand tight as another contraction rippled through her belly, her pallor and perspiration-covered face acting like a kick in the gut.

"You better remember that," she bit out, relaxing onto the pillows and easing her death grip on his hand as the contraction passed. "If this is only the beginning I feel a lot of swearing coming on, most of it directed at you for getting me into this predicament in the first place."

There was no malice behind her words. If anything, the cheeky glint in her eyes surprised him.

"As I recall, we were both involved at the time."

Their gazes locked as memories of their incredible night in Singapore washed over them, notching up the temperature in the birthing suite in an instant.

"We never got to finish our talk," she said, a small, serene smile playing about her lips, begging him to reach forward and cover them with his own.

However, another ripping contraction vanquished that urge and their shared moment of intimacy was lost.

Nate had never been a clock watcher, putting in the required hours at work without batting an eye, but over the next eight hours he couldn't tear his gaze away from the large, ugly kitchen clock stuck on the wall in front of him as he rubbed Kris's back, offered her ice chips to suck, and bore the brunt of her increasingly fraying temper.

"Nate, I don't think I can do this anymore..." Her whispered plea for reassurance slammed into him and his gut churned as he leaned forward and stroked her forehead, needing the physical contact for reassurance as much as she did.

"You're doing great, sweetheart. You're amazing. Hang in

there. Our daughter is on her way." He hated how inadequate he sounded, how totally pathetic, and he turned in desperation to the midwife as she entered the room, silently imploring her to give them good news.

The midwife, way too calm and cheery, bustled about with ferocious efficiency, before pronouncing Kris ten centimetres dilated. "There's a slight problem, dear."

Nate's heart stopped as he stared in open-mouthed horror at the midwife so casually delivering news that could be catastrophic. As he'd already learned, there were no 'slight' problems with birthing, they tended to be major ones, and he hoped this wasn't anything serious.

"Though the baby is head down, her head is facing the wrong way. In these cases, usually with a bit of pushing, the little mite will automatically turn and come out quickly. So we'll give it a go, shall we?"

"What's with the we business?" Kris muttered, sending the midwife one of the killer glares she'd been reserving for him.

In the midst of his anxiety, she managed to illicit a smile, albeit a weak one, and he copped an angry glare for his trouble too.

"You're almost there, sweetheart." He leaned over and kissed her cheek, half expecting her to push him away or whack him for his trouble. Instead, she surprised him by cupping his cheek for an all too brief instant before the next contraction took her breath away and the rollercoaster of pain began again.

And again...and again...Minutes turned into an interminable stretch of moans and groans as he helplessly watched the woman he loved go through unbearable agony.

He barely registered the midwife hooking up a foetal monitor over Kris's belly, he barely remembered passing Kris the nitrous oxide to help with the crest of the increasingly painful contractions, but when the baby's heart beat started to slow with every push, he rocketed out of the chair and marched across to the midwife in deep conversation with the obstetrician who'd just entered the room.

"You've got to do something now," he said, casting frantic glances back at Kris lying in a sweaty, pale, twisted heap on the bed, hating his helpless frustration more than anything.

"We're taking her to theatre shortly," the obstetrician said, giving him a comforting pat on the arm. "An anaesthetist is on their way up for the epidural and once that's administered we'll get things sped up."

"What's going on?" Kris's shout made them jump and he followed the obstetrician back to the bed, his eyes glued to the foetal monitor, petrified when the heart beat slowed yet again.

"We're taking you to theatre once you have an epidural. We don't let our mom's go longer than twenty-four hours and you've done a mighty job, Kris. However, this little girl of yours isn't turning so I'll try high forceps and if that doesn't work we'll be doing a Caesarean, okay?"

Nate expected Kris to protest, remembering how pro-natural she'd been about the birth throughout the ante-natal classes, but she merely nodded and slumped, exhaustion rendering her speechless.

"Let's do it, Doc," he said, grateful for some positive action, not quite believing Kris had been in labour for almost a day.

The rest happened in a blur: the trip down to theatre, gowning up himself, the obstetrician smiling when the forceps worked and asking Kris to give one last almighty push.

Nate's breath caught as the doctor held up a red-faced, screaming little girl covered in white gunk, and he would've forgotten how to breathe if Kris hadn't burst into noisy tears at that moment.

"She's beautiful, just like her mother," he whispered, tears filling his eyes as he swept aside the damp strands of hair stuck to Kris's face and kissing her on the mouth.

"Nate, look at her." Her sobs subsided but the tears continued, flowing down her cheeks as their bundled daughter was placed in her arms and his tears fell softly onto the baby's blanket. "She's incredible."

He leaned forward and cuddled them close, filled with an indescribable love for his girls.

"We never did get around to choosing a name," Kris said, nuzzling the top of the baby's head with her nose while he traced the soft curve of his daughter's cheek.

"Later," he said, wanting to capture this moment in time forever. "I love you both so much."

Thankfully, Kris didn't argue as they formed a protective circle around the baby with their linked hands.

Twenty-Six

Kristen pretended to sleep as Nate crept into her room and over to the cot, his voice barely a whisper as he greeted his daughter.

"Hey, little one. Hope you're being good for Mommy. She needs her rest and so do you."

He got that right. She hadn't had a moment's peace since the birth, with midwives teaching her to breastfeed, trying to express a non-existent milk supply, and learning how to bathe her gorgeous girl. Then there was Nate, always hanging around, doting over her and the baby, reminding her of how amazing he was and of what she couldn't have.

"You know, I bet your half-brother is looking down on you right now. He's your guardian angel."

She stiffened, wondering if the analgesia they'd given her for the episiotomy stitches had affected her comprehension.

"I never got to hold him like I've held you. Guess I was too heartbroken, but I've regretted it ever since. Babies need to be held and I promise to cuddle you every single day."

Kris opened her eyes, unable to lie there and pretend she hadn't heard the gut-wrenching pain in Nate's voice.

"You had a son?"

Nate jumped and swivelled to face her, his face cloaked in shadows. "I never got to that part, did I?"

He sat on the edge of the bed and took hold of her hand, glancing across at the cot with love radiating from his eyes.

"Tell me now," she said, happy to have her hand held, enthralled by the emotional bond created from having the man she loved stand by her through every second of the labour ordeal.

"You know Julia was pregnant when she died. I wanted to tell you the rest but I didn't want to scare you, what with the way she died." He shook his head. "I'd been away with work and came home to find her bleeding on the kitchen floor. She'd had a placental abruption and haemorrhaged quickly. They both died."

"Hell, Nate. I'd assumed it was a brain haemorrhage."

Now she understood his stricken expression when he'd hovered over her after she'd passed out on the stairs. He'd probably thought he was walking in on the same tragic scenario all over again.

"I blamed myself. If I'd been there for her, if I hadn't gone to work that day, maybe I could've done something and prevented their senseless deaths in some way, but I wasn't around and I'll never forgive myself for that." He looked away, his glassy stare fixed on some point over her shoulder and she remained silent, unsure what to say, knowing whatever words she mumbled would sound trite and inadequate. "I've lived with the guilt for a long time, shutting myself off from everything but work, focussing all my energy on business, trying to numb the pain by not stopping. Then you came along."

Dread crept through her exhausted body. He'd said he loved her before the birth and now she finally understood. Nate had shut down emotionally since losing Julia and their child, and she'd given him what he wanted most, another child, so he'd confused his awakening emotions with love.

He didn't love her, he couldn't. How could he love her when he was still grieving? He'd just said he could never forgive himself; how did he expect to ever move on?

"You don't have to explain anything to me, Nate. I get it."

"No, you don't. I've been battling the daily guilt of not being there for Julia but I've been fighting an added guilt too. The guilt of moving on, of letting Julia go, of possibly loving another woman, of acknowledging I love you more than I loved her."

Kristen's jaw dropped and she didn't resist when he reached up and tipped a finger under her chin to close it.

"I already told you Jules and I were high school sweethearts. It's only now I realise that our love was based on friendship rather than the inexplicable connection you and I've had since we first met. What I feel for you is richer, deeper, more profound, than anything I felt for Julia, and I've been beating myself up over it until I realised it's okay to love you, to feel good again, to start living my life rather than using my guilt as an excuse to push you away."

Hope unfurled in her heart, uncertain and fluttering and making her head feel lighter than any pain relief.

"I love you, Kris. You're everything to me."

His lips brushed hers, a gentle kiss of persuasion and promise, and she responded as if someone had lit a rocket under her, sliding her hands around his neck and pulling him up the bed, desperate to get closer, throwing all her pent-up emotions into the kiss she'd been waiting for; the incredibly special, once-in-a-lifetime kiss of a man who truly loved her.

"You know I love you too?" She traced his bottom lip with her fingertip, enjoying his blatant shock.

"I thought we had a few sparks and hoped you'd grow to love me?"

"Too late. It's already happened," she said, snapping her fingers and injecting all the love she had in heart for him into a dazzling smile. "Seems like I've loved you forever."

"Forever, huh?" Capturing her face in his hands, he brushed another tantalising kiss across her lips. "Sounds good to me. That's how long we've got to love each other, to create the happy family we deserve."

He'd said the magic words—love and happy family—and Kristen melted into his embrace, knowing there could be no better place than in his protective arms.

"You're going to marry me, right?"

Kristen pretended to think about it as Nate kissed his way slowly up her neck, stopping to lavish some extra attention on a sensitive spot.

"You can't keep me dangling forever, you know. I don't want to be proposing at Maeve's twenty-first."

She smiled. "You know I love that name, right? And it's so perfect to have our little girl named after your mom, especially as she'll never get to meet her grand-daughter."

A shadow flickered across Nate's dark eyes. "Mom would've loved her as much as we do. Now, stop trying to distract me by getting sentimental and tell me your answer."

"I thought I'd already answered you?"

She rubbed noses with him, loving their closeness, the teasing, the one hundred percent security being with a guy like him brought. For a girl who'd craved stability her whole life she'd finally found it, all wrapped up in one incredible package.

"You haven't given me an answer. What with you threatening to walk out on me after my first proposal, then scaring the life out of me by collapsing, closely followed by Maeve's birth just as I'm professing my undying love to you, we haven't got around to discussing the important stuff like weddings."

She knew he loved her sass, so she arched a brow in provocation. "So you're pretty confident there's going to be a wedding, huh?"

"You bet." His fingers skimmed her spine, his feather-light touch scattering goosebumps all over and she shivered, preening under his touch.

"In that case, who am I to stand in the way of your pushy nature?"

They grinned at each other like a couple head over heels in love, knowing there'd never been any doubt about getting married once they'd declared their love and enjoying playing the sparring game.

"Is it acceptable to marry the boss?"

"You're not my boss anymore," she said, pressing a slow kiss to his lips, the type of kiss guaranteed to light a fire between them. "I'm on maternity leave as of now, remember?"

His hands framed her face as the kiss ended, his dark eyes glowing with passion in the surreal dawn light. "I love you so much."

"Right back at you." Her eyes filled with tears and he wiped them away with a gentle fingertip.

"Still those damn hormones, huh?"

"Yeah. They make me do crazy things."

"As long as you don't fall out of love with me when they wear off, I'll be happy."

"Not a chance, my love."

"So do you want to wait until Maeve's walking so she can be flower-girl at our wedding?"

"Hell no. I need to make an honest man out of you ASAP."

"How soon?" He traced her cheek, toyed with a strand of hair, twisting it around his finger in the same way he'd done to the rest of her since the first moment she'd met him.

"I'm a busy mom. You're the high-flying CEO who plans

everything to the nth degree. How long do you think it will take to organise our wedding?"

His eyes glittered with intent as he tugged gently on the strand, bringing their lips an inch apart. "You'll be in hospital for five nights. So is a week from today too soon?"

"To start the rest of our lives together? Never," she said, closing the distance between them and kissing him until they were both panting and breathless.

When they finally eased apart, he said, "I'm kidding," desire clouding his eyes. "I'll give you a chance to catch your breath."

She smiled and dropped a kiss on his lips. "Soon is fine. A small ceremony with you, me and Maeve. Perfect."

"Perfect," he echoed, sliding his arms around her until she had no option but to snuggle tight against his chest, knowing she'd found what she'd always wanted.

Love, respect and validation, made all the more special by Maeve, their adorable baby girl sleeping peacefully by their side.

A family of her own.
Perfect indeed.

Thank you for taking the time to read this book and the Creative in Love series.

Every review counts so if you enjoyed this story, please consider leaving a review.

Read Nicola's newest feel-good romance DID NOT FINISH.
He's a bestselling author. She's a career-wrecking book reviewer. Who will lose the plot first?

Nicola has many more romances to choose from, including the Bashful Brides series.

Here's a snippet from NOT THE ROMANTIC KIND.

'WE HAVE a problem.'

Four words Rory Devlin did *not* want to hear, especially at his first Devlin Corp Shareholders' Ball.

He glanced around the Palladium ballroom to see everyone drinking, dining or dancing and no visible crisis in sight, before acknowledging the waiter hovering at his elbow.

'What kind of problem?'

The kid, barely out of school, took a backward step and Rory belatedly remembered to temper his tone. It wasn't the waiter's fault he'd been dealing with non-stop hold-ups on the Portsea project all day.

Attending this shindig was the last thing he wanted to do but it had been six months since he'd stepped into the CEO role, six months since he'd tried to rebuild what had once been Australia's premier property developer, six months of repairing the damage his dad had inflicted.

The waiter glanced over his shoulder and tugged nervously at his bow tie. 'You better see for yourself.'

Annoyed by the intrusion, Rory followed the waiter to a small annexe off the main foyer, where the official launch of the Portsea project would take place in fifteen minutes.

'She's in there,' the waiter said.

She?

Rory took one look inside the annexe and balked.

'I'll take it from here,' he said, and the waiter scuttled away before he'd finished speaking.

Squaring his shoulders, he tugged at the ends of his dinner jacket and strode into the room, eyeballing *the problem.*

Who eyeballed him back with a defiant tilt of her head, sending loose shoulder-length blonde waves tumbling around her heart-shaped face. She wore a smug smile along with a flimsy blue cocktail dress that matched her eyes.

He hoped the links around her wrists and ankles were the latest eccentric fashion accessory and not what he thought they were: chains anchoring her to the display he had to unveil shortly.

'Can I help you?'

'I'm counting on it.'

Her pink-glossed lips compressed as she sized him up, starting at his Italian handmade shoes and sweeping upwards in an all-encompassing stare that made him edgy.

'Shall we go somewhere and discuss?'

'Not possible.' She rattled the chains at her wrist and the display gave an ominous wobble. 'As you can see, I'm a bit tied up at the moment.'

He winced at her pitiful pun and she laughed.

'Not my best, but a girl has to do what a girl has to do to get results.'

He pointed at the steel links binding her to his prized display. 'And you think chaining yourself to my company's latest project is going to achieve your objective?'

'You're here, aren't you?'

What *was* this, some kind of revenge? He frowned, searching his memory banks. Was she someone he'd dated? A business associate? Someone he'd slighted in some way?

If she'd gone this far to get his attention, she wanted something. Something he'd never give, considering the way she'd gone about this. He didn't take kindly to threats or blackmail —or whatever *this* was.

Having some bold blonde wearing a dress that accentuated

rather than hid her assets, her long legs bare, and her toenails painted the same silver as her chains bail him up like this...no way in hell would he cave to her demands.

Maybe she wanted to sell him prime land? Put in a tender for a job? Supply and interior decorate the luxury mansions on the Portsea project? Too damn bad. She'd have to make an appointment like everyone else. This kind of stunt didn't impress him. Not one bit.

She chose that moment to shift her weight from one leg to the other, rattling the chains binding her slim ankles, drawing his attention to those long bare legs again.

His perfectly male response in studying their shape and the smoothness of her skin annoyed him as much as the time he was wasting standing here.

'You wanted to see *me* specifically?'

'If you're Rory Devlin, CEO of the company about to ruin the marine environment out near Portsea, then, yeah, you're the man I want to see.'

His heart sank. Since he'd taken over the reins at Devlin Corp he'd borne the brunt of every hippy lobbyist and environmentalist in town. None that looked quite as ravishing as the woman before him, but all of them demonstrated the same headstrong fanaticism.

Eco-nuts like her had almost derailed the company. Thankfully, he had a stronger backbone than his father, who'd dilly-dallied rather than made firm decisions on the Port Douglas project last year.

Devlin Corp had ensured the rainforest in far North Queensland would be protected, but that hadn't stopped zealot protestors stalling construction, costing millions and almost bankrupting the company in the process.

If Rory hadn't stepped in and played hardball he shuddered to think what would've happened to his family legacy.

'You've been misinformed. My company takes great pains

to ensure our developments blend with the environment, not ruin it.'

'Give me a break.' She rolled her eyes before focussing them on him with a piercing clarity that would've intimidated a lesser man. 'I've researched the land you develop, with those flashy houses you dump in the middle of nowhere and sell for a small fortune.'

She strained against her chains as if she'd like to jab him in the chest, and his gaze momentarily strayed to hers before her exasperated snort drew his attention upwards.

'Your developments slash trees and defile land and don't give a rat's ass about energy conservation—'

'Stop right there.'

He crossed the room to stand a foot in front of her, feeling vindicated when she had to tilt her head back to look up at him, and annoyed when a tantalising blend of sunshine, fresh grass and spring mornings wrapped around him.

'You're misinformed as well as trespassing. Unlock yourself. Now.'

Tiny sapphire flecks sparked in her eyes before her lips curved upwards in an infuriatingly smug smile.

'Can't do that.'

'Why?'

'Because you haven't agreed to my terms yet.'

He shook his head, pressing the pads of his fingers against his eyes. Unfortunately, when he opened them, she was still there.

'We do this the easy way or the hard way. Easy way, you unlock yourself. Hard way, I call Security and they use bolt cutters to humiliate you further.'

Her eyes narrowed, not dimming in brilliance one iota. 'Go ahead. Call them.'

Damn, she knew he was bluffing. No way would he draw attention to her and risk the shareholders getting curious.

'Give me the key.'

He took a step closer, deriving some satisfaction from the way she inhaled sharply and wriggled backwards before he realised his mistake. He'd wanted to intimidate her; he'd ended up being an inch away from her.

'Make me.' Her tongue darted out to moisten her bottom lip and he stared at it, shaken to the core by the insane urge to taste those lips for himself.

Hell.

He never backed down—ever. He'd taken on every challenge thrust upon him: changing schools in his mid-teens so he could be groomed to take over Devlin Corp one day, ousting his layabout father from the CEO role, stepping up when it counted and dragging an ailing company out of the red and into the black.

She wanted him to capitulate to her demands? As if.

'I'm not playing this game with you.' He used his frostiest, most commanding tone, the one he reserved for recalcitrant contractors who never failed to delay projects.

Predictably, it did little for the pest threatening to derail his evening.

She merely smiled wider. 'Why? Games can be fun.'

Exasperated beyond belief, he felt his fingers tingle with the urge to throttle her.

Dragging in deep, calming breaths, he stared at the model of Portsea Point, the largest project he'd undertaken since assuming CEO duties. He needed this project to fly. Needed it to be his biggest, boldest success to push the company back to its rightful place: at the top of Australia's luxury property developers.

If he could nail this development, business would flood in, and Devlin Corp would shrug off the taint his father had besmirched the company with in his short stint as CEO.

Failure was not an option.

He glanced at his watch and grimaced. The unveiling would take place in less than ten minutes and he needed to get rid of this woman pronto.

Thrusting his hands into his pockets and out of strangling distance, he squared his shoulders and edged back to tower over her.

'What do you want?'

'Thought you'd never ask.'

His gaze strayed to her glossed lips again and he mentally kicked himself.

'I want a little one-on-one time with you.'

'There are easier ways to get a date.'

Confusion creased her brow for a second, before her eyes widened in horror. 'I don't want a *date* with you.'

She made it sound as if he'd offered her some one-on-one time with a nest of vipers.

'Sure? I come highly recommended.'

'I bet,' she muttered, glancing away, but not before he'd seen the flare of interest in her eyes.

'In fact, I can give you the numbers of half the Melbourne female population who could verify exactly how great a date I am and—'

'Half of Melbourne?' She snorted. 'Don't flatter yourself.'

Leaning into her personal space, he savoured her momentary flare of panic as she eased away. 'You're the one who wanted one-on-one time with me.'

'For an interview, you idiot.'

Ah...so that's what this stunt was about. An out-of-work environmentalist after a job.

He had two words for her: hell, no.

But against his better judgement he admired her sass. Most jobseekers would apply through an agency or harass his PA for an appointment. Not many would go to this much trouble.

He crooked his finger and she warily eased forward.

'Here's a tip. You want an interview? Don't go calling your prospective boss nasty names.'

'Idiot isn't nasty. If I wanted nasty I would've gone with bast—'

'Unbelievable.'

His jaw ached with the effort not to laugh. If his employees had half the chutzpah this woman did Devlin Corp would be number one again in next to no time.

'What do you say? Give me fifteen minutes of your time and I'll ensure you won't regret it.'

She punctuated her plea with a toss of her shoulder-length blonde hair and once again the tempting fragrance of spring outdoors washed over him.

He opened his mouth to refuse, to tell her exactly what he thought of her underhand tricks.

'I don't want to disrupt your Portsea project. I want to help you.' She eyeballed him, her determination and boldness as attractive as the rest of her. 'In the marine environmental field, I'm the best there is.'

Worn down by her admirable persistence, and a desire to get her out of here before any of the shareholders wandered in early for the unveiling, he found himself nodding.

'You've got fifteen minutes.'

'Deal.' Her triumphant grin turned sly. 'Now, if you don't mind fishing the key out of its hiding spot, I'll get out of your way.'

'Hiding spot?'

Her gaze dropped to her cleavage.

His blood pounded in his ears as he imagined reaching into her cleavage for the key. Could this evening get any crazier?

'Uh...okay.'

He reached a tentative hand towards her chest when she let out a howl of laughter that had him leaping backwards.

'Don't worry, I've got it.'

With a few deft flicks of her wrists she'd slipped out of her chains and kicked the ones around her ankles free.

'You set me up.'

He should've been angry, should have cancelled her interview on the spot. Instead, he found himself watching her as she deftly wound the chains and stuffed them into a sparkly hold-all she'd hidden under the table, wondering what she'd come up with next to surprise him.

'I didn't set you up so much as have a little fun at your expense.' She patted his chest. 'I snuck a peek at you earlier in the ballroom and it looked like you could do with a little lightening up.'

Speechless, he wondered why he was putting up with her pushiness. He didn't take that from anyone—ever.

She pressed a business card into his hand and the simple touch of her palm against his fired a jolt of awareness he hadn't expected or wanted.

'My details are all there. I'll call to set up that interview.'

She slung her bag over her shoulder, the rattle of chains a reminder of the outlandishness of this evening.

'Nice to meet you, Rory Devlin.'

With a crisp salute she sauntered out the door, leaving him gobsmacked.

Read NOT THE ROMANTIC KIND now!

FREE BOOK AND MORE

SIGN UP TO NICOLA'S NEWSLETTER for a free book!

Read Nicola's feel-good romance **DID NOT FINISH**

Or her gothic suspense novels **THE RETREAT** and **THE HAVEN**

(The gothic prequel **THE RESIDENCE** is free!)

Try the **CARTWRIGHT BROTHERS** duo

FASCINATION

PERFECTION

The **WORKPLACE LIAISONS** duo

THE BOSS

THE CEO

The **REDEEMING A BAD BOY** series

THE REBEL

THE PLAYER

THE WANDERER

THE CHARMER

THE EX (releasing September 2024)

THE FRIEND (releasing October 2024

Try the **BASHFUL BRIDES** series

NOT THE MARRYING KIND

NOT THE ROMANTIC KIND

NOT THE DARING KIND

NOT THE DATING KIND

The **CREATIVE IN LOVE** series

THE GRUMPY GUY

THE SHY GUY

THE GOOD GUY

Try the **BOMBSHELLS** series

BEFORE (FREE!)

BRASH

BLUSH

BOLD

BAD

BOMBSHELLS BOXED SET

The **WORLD APART** series

WALKING THE LINE (FREE!)

CROSSING THE LINE

TOWING THE LINE

BLURRING THE LINE

WORLD APART BOXED SET

The **HOT ISLAND NIGHTS** duo

WICKED NIGHTS

WANTON NIGHTS

The **ROMANCE CYNICS** duo

CUPID SEASON

SORRY SEASON

The **BOLLYWOOD BILLIONAIRES** series

FAKING IT

MAKING IT

The **LOOKING FOR LOVE** series

LUCKY LOVE

CRAZY LOVE

SAPPHIRES ARE A GUY'S BEST FRIEND

THE SECOND CHANCE GUY

Check out Nicola's website for a full list of her books.

And read her other romances as Nikki North.

'MILLIONAIRE IN THE CITY' series.

LUCKY

FANCY

FLIRTY

FOLLY

MADLY

Check out the **ESCAPE WITH ME** series.
TRUST ME
FORGIVE ME

Try the **LAW BREAKER** series
THE DEAL MAKER
THE CONTRACT BREAKER

About the Author

USA TODAY bestselling and multi-award winning author Nicola Marsh writes page-turning fiction to keep you up all night.

She's published 86 books and sold millions of copies worldwide.

She currently writes contemporary romance and domestic suspense.

She's also a Waldenbooks, Bookscan, Amazon, iBooks and Barnes & Noble bestseller, a RBY (Romantic Book of the Year) and National Readers' Choice Award winner, and a multi-finalist for a number of awards including the Romantic Times Reviewers' Choice Award, HOLT Medallion, Booksellers' Best, Golden Quill, Laurel Wreath, and More than Magic.

A physiotherapist for thirteen years, she now adores writing full time, raising her two dashing young heroes, sharing fine food with family and friends, and her favorite, curling up with a good book!